MYSTERY IN WHITE

A CHRISTMAS CRIME STORY

MYSTERY IN WHITE

A CHRISTMAS CRIME STORY

J. JEFFERSON FARJEON

WITH AN INTRODUCTION BY
MARTIN EDWARDS

THE BRITISH LIBRARY

This edition published in 2014 by
The British Library
96 Euston Road
London NW1 2DB

Originally published in London in 1937 by Wright & Brown

Cataloguing in Publication Data
A catalogue record for this book is available from the British Library

ISBN 978 0 7123 5770 8

Typeset by IDSUK (DataConnection) Ltd
Printed and bound by CPI Group (UK) Ltd, Croydon, CR0 4YY

CONTENTS

INTRODUCTION

MARTIN EDWARDS

Mystery in White is an entertaining story of crime at Christmas, written by an author who – although today little-known – was a major figure during the Golden Age of murder between the two world wars. No less an authority than Dorothy L. Sayers pronounced that 'Jefferson Farjeon is quite unsurpassed for creepy skill in mysterious adventures', and the storyline of *Mystery in White* allows him ample scope to demonstrate that skill.

The set-up is enticing, if superficially familiar. A strange assortment of passengers travelling by train during a blizzard find themselves caught in an acute dilemma when the track becomes impassable. Yet despite some similarity in the initial set-up, Farjeon's story, first published in 1937, really owes nothing in terms of structure or solution to Agatha Christie's classic *Murder on the Orient Express*, which appeared three years earlier. This time, the locale is not a remote part of continental Europe, but the English countryside, and the train is not the legendary and luxurious trans-continental express, but a third-class compartment on the 11.37 from St Pancras (or should that be Euston? both those great stations are mentioned in the very first chapter.)

Having created expectations in the reader of one kind of detective story, Farjeon promptly disrupts them by directing events down a very different track. Above all, this is not a whodunit set *on* a train, and the plot thickens like the snow once a small group of travellers abandon the security of their carriage to trudge through the 'strange fairyland' outside. Spotting a lonely house, they ring the bell, but receive no answer. The door is unlocked, and when they venture inside, they discover that a fire is burning, and tea has been laid. Yet the place appears to be deserted, and events take an increasingly sinister turn after the arrival of a mysterious Cockney who says his name is Smith

Rather than following in Christie's footsteps, Farjeon was, in fact, anticipating the *mise en scène* of her short story 'Three Blind Mice', which was published almost a decade after this book, and later adapted into that classic stage mystery, *The Mousetrap*. The cosy yet spooky setting of a country house, cut off from the out-side world by deep snow, is a superbly atmospheric backdrop for a murder story, and Farjeon uses it to good effect. His main characters are nicely differentiated, and include a chorus girl, an elderly bore, and Mr Edward Maltby of the Royal Psychical Society, as well as the brother and sister who are the lead pro-tagonists. The narrative twists and turns so that the reader never quite knows what to expect next. This combination of pleasing ingredients makes for a light and agreeable read.

Mystery in White is the work of a capable writer at the height of his powers. By the time it arrived on the shelves, Farjeon had published more than two dozen novels, the most famous of which was *No. 17*. Originally a stage play, this story provided the basis for Alfred Hitchcock's *Number Seventeen*, a film thriller from 1932. The movie is not one that the Master of Suspense remembered fondly; he told François Truffaut that it was a 'dis-aster', and felt the core elements were too clichéd. For his part, Farjeon quietly perfected the marriage in his fiction of genial humour with suspense and action, and earned considerable acclaim in a literary career lasting for more than thirty years.

Joseph Jefferson Farjeon (1883–1955), known to those close to him as Joe, came from a family of high achievers in the world of popular culture. His first names came from his grandfather, the

American actor Joseph Jefferson, whose most famous role was Rip Van Winkle. Jefferson's daughter Maggie married Benjamin Farjeon, who had been born in Whitechapel to an impoverished family of Jewish immigrants, and became a prolific and successful novelist. In addition to Joe, their children included Harry, a composer, Herbert, a drama critic and director, and Eleanor, a renowned author of poetry, memoirs and stories for young people, who also wrote the words of 'Morning Has Broken', a hymn which after her death became a Top Ten hit for Cat Stevens.

When writing *No. 17*, Joe gave his father's first name to a tramp with a penchant for trouble and a taste for amateur detection. Ben the tramp later appeared in a string of novels such as *Ben on the Job* (1932), one of surprisingly few Farjeon titles to have been reprinted during the past thirty years. Ben is a likeable character, and so, by all accounts, was his creator. For all the chill of the Christmas-time snow in *Mystery in White*, there are repeated clues to Farjeon's amiable personality in the good humour that shines through from start to finish. Towards the end of the book, a police inspector, belatedly arrived on the scene, exclaims, 'Four murders in a dozen hours! I reckon I've earned my bit of turkey.' But the official version of events is not necessarily the whole truth, and this is yet another reason why it is so good to see this enjoyable Yuletide yarn back in print after many years of undeserved neglect.

CHAPTER I

THE SNOWBOUND TRAIN

THE Great Snow began on the evening of December 19th. Shoppers smiled as they hurried home, speculating on the chances of a White Christmas. Their hopes were dampened when they turned on their wireless to learn from the smooth impersonal voice of the B.B.C. announcer that an anti-cyclone was callously wending its way from the North-West of Ireland; and on the 20th the warmth arrived, turning the snow to drizzle and the thin white crust to muddy brown.

"Not this year!" sighed the disappointed sentimentalists as they slipped sadly through the slush.

But on the 21st the snow returned, this time in earnest. Brown became white again. The sounds of traffic were deadened. Wheel marks, foot marks, all marks, were blotted out as soon as they were made. The sentimentalists rejoiced.

It snowed all day and all night. On the 22nd it was still snowing. Snowballs flew, snowmen grew. Sceptical children regained their belief in fairyland, and sour adults felt like Santa Claus, buying more presents than they had ever intended. In the evening the voice of the announcer, travelling through endless white ether, informed the millions that more snow was coming. The anti-cyclone from the North-West of Ireland had got lost in it.

More snow came. It floated down from its limitless source like a vast extinguisher. Sweepers, eager for their harvest, waited in vain for the snow to stop. People wondered whether it would ever stop.

It grew beyond the boundaries of local interest. By the 23rd it was news. By the 24th it was a nuisance. Practical folk cursed. Even the sentimentalists wondered how they were going to carry out their programmes. Traffic was dislocated. Cars and motor-coaches lost themselves. Railway gangs fought snowdrifts. The thought of the thaw, with its stupendous task of conversion, became increasingly alarming.

The elderly bore, however, who formed one of half a dozen inmates of a third-class compartment on the 11.37 from Euston, refused to be alarmed. In fact, although the train had come to an unofficial halt that appeared to be permanent, he pooh-poohed the whole thing as insignificant with the irritating superiority of a world-traveller.

"If you want to know what snow's *really* like," he remarked to the young lady next to him, "you ought to try the Yukon."

"Ought I?" murmured the young lady obediently.

She was a chorus girl, and her own globe-trotting had been limited to the provincial towns. Her present destination was Manchester, which in this weather seemed quite far enough off.

"I remember once, in Dawson City, we had a month of snow," the bore went on, while the young man on his other side thought, "My God, is he starting off again?" "It was in '99. No, '98. Well, one or the other. I was a kid at the time. We got sick of the damn stuff!"

"Well, I'm sick of this damn stuff," answered the chorus girl, twisting her head towards the window. All she saw was a curtain of white flakes. "How much longer are we going to wait here, does anybody think? We must have stopped an hour."

"Thirty-four minutes," corrected the tall, pale youth opposite, with a glance at his wrist-watch. He did not have spots, but looked as though he ought to have had. His unhealthy complexion was due partly to the atmosphere of the basement office in which he worked, and partly to a rising temperature. He ought to have been in bed.

"Thank you," smiled the chorus girl. "I see one's got to be careful when you're around!"

The clerk smiled faintly. He was impressed by the chorus girl's beauty. A real, die-hard platinum blonde. Marvellous person to take out to supper, if one had the courage for that sort of thing. He believed the bore would have had the courage and had noted the man's quick little, half-sly glances between his egotistical statements. He even believed the chorus girl might accept an invitation. There was something vulnerable about her which her assurance attempted to cloak. But the clerk was even more impressed by the other young lady in the compartment, the one who was sitting on the other side of the bore. To take *her* out to supper would provide more than a momentary thrill; it would entirely upset one's work. She was dark. She had a tall, supple figure. (The chorus girl was rather small.) He felt sure she played a good game of tennis, swam and rode. He visualised her cantering over moors and sailing over five-barred gates, with her brother trying vainly to catch her up. Her brother was sitting in the corner opposite her. You knew it was her brother from their conversation, and you could also see it from their resemblance. They called each other David and Lydia.

Lydia was the next to speak.

"This is getting the limit!" she exclaimed. Her voice had a low, rich quality. "What about interviewing the guard again and asking if there's any hope of moving before next June?"

"I asked him ten minutes ago," said the bore. "I won't repeat what he said!"

"Not necessary," yawned David. "We have imaginations."

"Yes, and it seems we'll need our imaginations to-night!" chimed in the chorus girl. "*I'll* have to imagine I'm in Manchester!"

"Will you? *We* shall have to imagine we are at a Christmas house-party," smiled Lydia, "sleeping on downy beds. By the way, if we're in for an all-night session I hope the railway company will supply hot-water bottles!" Suddenly she caught the clerk's eye. She surprised the admiration in it, and was kind. "What will *you* have to imagine?" she asked. The catastrophe of the snow-drift and the camaraderie of Christmas were loosening tongues. The bore alone had needed no encouragement.

The clerk coloured, though his cheeks were already flushed with fever.

"Eh? Oh! An aunt," he jerked.

"If she's like mine, she's best left to the imagination!" laughed Lydia. "But then she probably isn't."

The clerk's aunt was not like Lydia's aunt. She was even more trying. But her dutiful nephew visited her periodically, partly for the sake of his financial future, and partly because he had a secret weakness for lonely people.

A little silence fell upon the party. The only one who thought it mattered was the chorus girl. A nervous restlessness possessed her soul, and she declared afterwards that she was sure she had been the first to move unconsciously into the shadow of coming events. "Because, goodness, I was all on edge," she said, "and why should I have been, I mean nothing had happened yet, and so far the old man in the corner hadn't opened his mouth. I don't believe he'd even opened his eyes, he might have been dead. And then, don't forget, he was right opposite me! And they say I'm psychic."

But her vague anticipations were not centred solely in the old man in the corner. She, too, had noticed the quick little, half-sly glances of the elderly bore, who, as she knew, was not too elderly to think about her in a certain way. She had also noticed the clerk's eyes upon her leg, and the rather studious avoidance of any such vulgar interest on the part of the other young man. If Jessie Noyes was very conscious of her physical attractions she claimed it was her business to be. She was well aware of both her power and the limitation of her power, and while the power, despite its small thrills, gave her a secret dread, the limitation was a secret sorrow. How wonderful to be able to conquer a man wholly and eternally, instead of being just an ephemeral taste! Still, she was not bitter. She was anxious and nervous and warm. Life was life....

Driven now by her restlessness, and finding the silence unendurable, she broke it by suddenly exclaiming:

"Well, let's go on! That's only four of us! What will *you* have to imagine?"

The question was addressed, not too wisely, to the bore.

"Me? Imagine?" he answered. "I don't know it's my habit to imagine. Take things as they come—good, bad, or indifferent—that's my motto. You learn that when you've knocked around as I have."

"Perhaps I can be more interesting," said the old man in the corner, opening his eyes suddenly.

He was neither dead nor asleep. As a matter of fact, he had heard every word that had been uttered since the train had steamed out of Euston at 11.37, and the probability of this made more than one of the five people who now turned to him feel a little uncanny. Not that he had heard anything he should not have heard; but a man who listens with his eyes closed, and whose eyes themselves become so peculiarly alive when they are opened—these eyes were like little lamps illuminating things invisible to others—is not the best tonic for frayed nerves.

"Please do, sir," answered David, after a short pause. "And invent a really good story for us—ours have been most definitely dull."

"Oh, mine is interesting without any invention," replied the old man, "and also, incidentally, rather appropriate to the season. I am on my way to interview King Charles the First."

"Really! With head, or without?" inquired David politely.

"With, I trust," the old man responded. "I am informed he is quite complete. We are to meet in an old house at Naseby. Frankly I am not very confident that the interview will occur. Charles the First may be bashful, or he may turn out to be just some ordinary cavalier hiding from Cromwell and Fairfax. After three hundred years, identity becomes a trifle confused." He smiled with cynical humour. "Or, again, he may be—*non est*. Simply the imagination of certain nervous people who think they have seen him about. But, of course," he added, after pursing his thin lips, "there is some possibility that he really is about. Yes, yes; if that over-maligned and over-glorified monarch *did* visit the house on the day of his defeat, and if the house's walls have stored up any emotional incidents that I can set free, we may add an interesting page to our history."

"Don't think me rude," exclaimed Lydia, "but do you really and truly believe in that sort of thing?"

"Exactly what do you mean by 'that sort of thing'?" asked the old man.

His tone was disapproving. The elderly bore took up the battle.

"Spooks and ghosts!" he grunted. "Pooh, I say! Stuff and nonsense! I've seen the Indian rope trick—yes, *and* exploded it! In Rangoon. '23."

"Spooks and ghosts," repeated the old man, his disapproval now diverted to the bore. The guard's voice sounded from a corridor in the distance. Though faint, the source of that was solid enough. "H'm—terms are deceptive. The only true language has no words, which explains, sir, why some people who speak too many words have no understanding."

"Eh?"

"Now if, by your expression spooks and ghosts, you imply conscious emanations, aftermaths of physical existence capable of independent functioning of a semi-earthly character, well, then I probably do not believe in that sort of thing. There are others, of course, whose opinions I respect, who disagree with me. They consider that you, sir, are doomed to exist perpetually in some form or other. That is, perhaps, a depressing thought. But if, by spooks and ghosts, you imply emanations recreated by acute living sensitiveness or intelligence from the inexhaustible store-houses of the past, then I do believe in that sort of thing. Inevitably."

The elderly bore was temporarily crushed. So was the chorus girl. But the brother and sister, anxious to be *au fait* with every phase of progressive thought, if only to discard it, and equipped with sufficient fortitude to withstand its shocks, were intrigued.

"Reduced to words of not more than two syllables," said David, "you mean we can conjure up the past?"

"Conjure up is not a happy term," answered the old man. "It suggests magic, and there is nothing magical in the process. We can reveal—expose—the past. The past is ineradicable."

"Bosh!" exclaimed the bore.

He did not like being crushed. The old man who had crushed him bent forward to repeat the operation.

"What is a simple gramophone record but a record of the past?" he demanded, tapping the bore on the knee. "Caruso is dead, but we can hear his voice to-day. This is not due to invention, but to discovery, and if the discovery had occurred three hundred years ago I should not have to travel to Naseby to hear Charles the First's voice—if, that is, I am to hear it. But Nature does not wait upon our discoveries. That is a thing so many ignoramuses forget. Her sound-waves, light-waves, thought-waves, emotional-waves—to mention a few of those which come within the limited range of our particular senses and perceptions—all travel ceaselessly, some without interruption, some to find temporary prisons in the obstructions where they embed themselves. Here they may diminish into negligible influences, or—mark this—they may be freed again. The captured waves, of course, are merely a fragment from the original source. Potentially everything that has ever existed, everything born of the senses, can be recovered by the senses. Fortunately, sir, there will be no gramophone record of your recent expletive; nevertheless, in addition to its mere mark on memory, your 'Bosh' will go on for ever."

The bore, rather surprisingly, put up a fight, though it was something in the nature of a death struggle.

"Then here is another Bosh to keep it company!" he snapped.

"You need never fear for the loneliness of your words," replied the old man.

"And what about your words?"

"They will go on, too. But it is unlikely that any future generation will recapture our present conversation. In spite of our obvious distaste for each other, our emotions are hardly virile enough. They will soon fade even from our own memories. But suppose—yes, sir, suppose they suddenly grow explosive? Suppose you leap upon me with a knife, plunging it into the heart of Mr. Edward Maltby, of the Royal Psychical Society, then indeed some future person sitting in this corner may become uncomfortably aware of a very unpleasant emotion."

He closed his eyes again; but his five travelling-companions all received the impression that he was still seeing them through his lids. The solid guard, passing along the corridor at that moment, was turned to with relief, although he had no comfort to offer.

"I'm afraid I can't say anything," he replied to inquiries, repeating a formula of which he was weary. "We're doing all we can, but with the line blocked before and behind, well, there it is."

"I call it disgraceful!" muttered the bore. "Where's the damned breakdown gang or whatever they call themselves?"

"We're trying to get assistance, we can't do more," retorted the guard.

"How long do you expect we'll stick here?"

"I'd like to know that myself, sir."

"All night?" asked Lydia.

"Maybe, miss."

"Can one walk along the line?"

"Only for a bit. It's worse beyond."

"Oh, dear!" murmured the chorus girl. "I must get to Manchester!"

"I asked because I was wondering whether there was another line or station near here," said Lydia.

"Well, there's Hemmersby," answered the guard. "That's a branch line that joins this at Swayton; but I wouldn't care to try it, not this weather."

"It's this weather that gives us the incentive," David pointed out. "How far is Hemmersby?"

"I shouldn't care to say. Five or six miles, p'r'aps."

"Which way?"

The guard pointed out of the corridor window.

"Yes, but we couldn't carry our trunks!" said Lydia. "What would happen to them?"

The guard gave a little shrug. Madness was not his concern, and he came across plenty.

"They would go on to their destination," he replied, "but I couldn't say when they'd turn up."

"According to you," smiled David, "they'd turn up before we would."

"Well, there you are," said the guard.

Then he continued on his way, dead sick of it.

There was a little silence. Lydia turned her head from the corridor and stared out of the window next to her.

"Almost stopped," she announced. "Well, people, what about it."

"Almost is not quite," answered her brother cautiously.

A second little silence followed. Jessie Noyes gazed at the tip of her shoe, fearful to commit herself. The flushed clerk seemed in the same condition. The bore's expression, on the other hand, was definitely unfavourable.

"Asking for trouble," he declared, when no one else spoke. "If none of you have been lost in a snowstorm, I have."

"Ah, but that was in Dawson City," murmured David, "where snow *is* snow."

Then a startling thing happened. The old man in the corner suddenly opened his eyes and sat upright. He stared straight ahead of him, but Jessie, who was in his line of vision, was convinced that he was not seeing her. A moment later he swerved round towards the corridor. Beyond the corridor window something moved; a dim white smudge that faded out into the all-embracing snow as they all watched it.

"The other line—yes, yes, quite a good idea," said the old man. "A merry Christmas to you all!"

He seized his bag from the rack, leapt across the corridor, jumped from the train, and in a few seconds he, too, had faded out.

"There goes a lunatic," commented the elderly bore, "if there ever was one!"

CHAPTER II

THE INVISIBLE TRACK

"WELL, what do we all make of it?" inquired David after a pause.

"I've already given you my opinion," responded the bore, and repeated it by tapping his forehead.

"Yes, but I'm afraid I daren't agree with the opinion, in case others follow the alleged lunatic's example," answered David. "You'll remember, we were just discussing what he has now done."

"Only we wouldn't do it quite so violently," interposed Lydia. "I almost thought for a moment that he'd spotted Charles the First!"

She spoke lightly, but she was watching to see how the others took her remark.

"Charles the Fiddlesticks!" muttered the bore.

"Didn't Nero use the fiddlesticks?" said David. "Anyhow, *somebody* was outside there before he hopped on to the line, so even if the going isn't good it can't be impossible." He turned to Jessie Noyes. "How do you feel about it?"

Jessie looked out of the window. The snow had ceased falling, and the motionless white scene was like a film that had suddenly stopped.

"I don't know," she replied. "I—I can't think what'll happen if I don't get to Manchester."

"It's important, is it?"

"Oh, yes!"

David glanced at his sister, and she nodded.

"We'll go, if you go," he said.

"But you mustn't go for me!" exclaimed Jessie quickly.

"It would only be partly for you," explained Lydia. "I really think we'd be using you as an excuse. You see, *we* want those nice downy beds! And then," she added, half-hesitatingly, "there's another thing. It least—it occurred to me."

"What?" asked David.

"I dare say it's quite ridiculous," she answered, "but somehow or other I can't help feeling just a bit worried about that Mr.—what was it? Maltby?"

"Edward Maltby, of the Royal Psychical Society," nodded David.

"He was such an old man! What'd we feel like if we read in to-morrow's papers that he'd been found buried in snow!"

"To-morrow's Christmas, and there won't be any papers," her brother pointed out.

"That doesn't reduce his chance of being buried in the snow, my darling," Lydia retorted.

Jessie chimed in, now seeking her own excuse:

"Yes, one does almost feel as if one almost ought to go after him, doesn't one?"

"This one doesn't," replied the bore, unconsciously adding a point in favour of departure.

Jessie's real excuse was that on the morrow a theatrical manager would have left Manchester, taking the chance of an engagement with him, and the possibility of missing both was emphasised by the voice of the guard when he returned along the corridor, answering questions that were flung at him as he went: "I'm sorry, sir, I can't say." "No, madam, nothing yet." "Yes, sir, it *may* be all night."

"Oh, *let's*!" cried Lydia.

"I'll—I'll join you, if I might," added the clerk with stammering boldness. "Make up a party, you know."

The tide of adventure was flowing fast. Lydia was already on her feet, bringing down her small suitcase. Had she known the suitcase's destination she would have hesitated. Only the elderly bore frowned.

"You're not really going, are you?" he asked the chorus girl.

"Why not, if they are?" she replied.

"Well, you take my advice, and stay here—with me?"

With the blindness of egotism, he was quite unconscious that his remark settled the matter.

Glad to be rid of his company, and armed with their small luggage, the four adventurers lowered themselves to the thick carpet of snow. Then David reached up and banged the door to—the corridor was fast filling with interested spectators—and the journey through strange fairyland began.

It began with disarming ease. Had difficulties arisen at once they might have returned, although pride would have rebelled against retreat at this early stage, and the vision of the bore's triumphant expression was another deterrent factor. Following Mr. Maltby's deep footprints for a few yards along the track, they came to a path bearing away from the line into the white distance. The line of the path was almost obliterated, but they identified it by a fence and a signpost: "Footpath to Hemmersby." This was evidently a point at which, in normal times, pedestrians crossed the railway.

The fence soon came to an end. The path lost its identifying boundary, and presumably continued diagonally across a field. Maltby's footprints and something that looked like a road beyond a distant hedge maintained the party's hope, but when they reached the thing that looked like a road to find that it belied its appearance, hope grew a little less.

"I—I suppose we're right?" queried Jessie.

"We must be," replied David cheerfully. "Follow the foot-prints!"

"The footprints mightn't be right," said the clerk.

"What depressing logic!" exclaimed David. "By the way, I sup-pose you've all noticed that we're following more than one set?"

"Yes, so the other man couldn't have been Charles the First," added Lydia, "because ghosts don't have footprints. Come on! I want to get somewhere!"

They continued on their uncertain way. While crossing a second field the snow began again. Each of the four travellers wondered whether to suggest going back, and each lacked the moral courage to put the wonder into words.

The second field sloped down into a small valley. Suddenly David gave a shout. He had ploughed a little way ahead.

"The road, people, the road!" he called.

They overtook him to find him staring disconsolately at a long, narrow ditch. Camouflaged by the snow, it had continued the story of deception.

"When you and I are all alone, David," said Lydia, "I'll tell you what I think of you!"

"Which way now?" asked Jessie, struggling against panic.

They stared around. The increasing snow had almost obliter-ated the marks of their predecessors. Just beyond the ditch they were being rapidly wiped out.

"What about *back*?" proposed David, voicing sense at last.

They turned. The slope they had descended was scarcely visible through the curtain of whirling white, and while they stood hesitating their own footprints became lost in the new covering.

"Yes, back!" cried Lydia. "That beastly bore was right!"

She began running. A voice hailed her immediately.

"Hey! Not that way!" called David.

Then they started arguing about the direction, while the thickening flakes blotted out all but themselves.

In the end they decided that it was as hopeless to attempt to return as to go forward. They skirted the ditch, blundered through an area of trees, crossed another field, descended into another valley, and walked into another ditch. Three breathless figures scrambled out on the farther side unaided. The fourth, Jessie, had to be lugged out.

"I say, are you hurt?" asked David anxiously.

"No, not a bit," answered Jessie, swaying.

He caught her unconscious form just before it slid to the ground, and a situation which had been bad enough already became suddenly worse. Lydia hurried to his side.

"What's the matter?" she exclaimed.

"The poor thing's conked out," he replied. "I say, Lydia, now we've just *got* to find somewhere!"

"Can you carry her?"

"She's light."

"Then come along. It won't help standing here. Where's that other man?"

His voice sounded as she spoke. The clerk had vanished, but now a muffled shout came through the white curtain.

"Hi! A gate!"

Lifting the unconscious figure in his arms, and telling his sister to take the suitcase she had dropped, David hastened towards the voice. He searched in vain for the origin.

"Where've you got to?" he called. "Shout again!"

The next instant the clerk loomed before him, and they almost collided.

"Good Lord!" gasped the clerk, staring at David's burden. "Is she bad?"

"Hope not; she just went off," answered David. "Where's this gate?"

"Just behind me. I think it leads somewhere."

At another time David would have commented that gates generally did lead somewhere, but he was not in a mood now for sarcasm or badinage.

"Shove it open," he said.

"It won't open," returned the clerk. "The snow's half-way to the top."

"Damn! Well, we'll have to climb it. Get over first, will you, and I'll pass her over to you. Think you can manage?"

"Yes, of course."

"You hop over, too, Lydia, and help him."

They managed somehow. Beyond the gate, David took the chorus girl again, with the snow almost up to his knees. The snow was rising like a tide, and every yard seemed more difficult than the last.

"If you ask me," murmured Lydia, dragging a sopping leg out of a small white pit, "I think the unconscious lady is having the best of it!"

"She won't when she comes to," answered David.

"All correct to instruct me," smiled Lydia.

"Did she fall down?" inquired the clerk.

"We all fell down," David reminded him, "but she seems to have fallen the hardest."

Round a bend—the lane was full of bends—an incident occurred that brought both alarm and hope. A mass of snow nearly enveloped them. It was like a miniature avalanche, and

it came sweeping down from nowhere. Warned by the preliminary swishing sound David and Lydia managed to evade it, but
the clerk was less lucky. For a second he disappeared, and then
emerged from an untidy white mound, spluttering.

"Where did *that* come from?" cried David.

"A roof, I should think," answered Lydia.

"Let's hope so!" replied David devoutly. "Have a look round,
you two, will you? I'm afraid the pack horse isn't quite so mobile.
But *prenez garde!*"

He stood still while they searched, holding his burden close
to him to give it warmth. In a few moments they reported a
barn.

"Splendid!" exclaimed David. "That's first-class news! Barns
don't grow all by themselves! We'll strike a house now before we
know it."

"A house!" repeated Lydia, with almost delirious ecstasy. "I'd
forgotten there were such things! A house—with a fire—and a
bath! Oh, a bath!"

"Sounds good," chattered the clerk.

With renewed hope they resumed their difficult way. They
twisted round another bend. On either side of them great white
trees rose, and the foliage increased. Once they walked into
the foliage. Then the lane dipped. This was unwelcome, for it
appeared to increase the depth of the snow and to augment the
sense that they were enclosed in it. With their retreat cut off,
they were advancing into a white prison.

The atmosphere became momentarily stifling. Then, suddenly,
the clerk gave a shout.

"What? Where?" cried David.

"Here; the house!" gulped the clerk.

Almost blinded by the whirling snowflakes, he had lowered his head; and when the building loomed abruptly in his path he only just saved himself from colliding with the front door.

CHAPTER III

STRANGE SANCTUARY

THE ringing of the bell brought no response. Knocking proved equally fruitless. For a short while it seemed as though they were doomed to further disappointment, although David was in a mood to break windows if the necessity arose. Then Lydia took the bull by the horns and tried the doorhandle. It turned, and she shoved the door open with a little sigh of relief. A roof, even without the invitation to stay beneath it, had become an urgent necessity.

They looked into a comfortable, spacious hall. It was early afternoon, and the light had not yet begun to fade noticeably, but the hall glowed with a queer white dimness, reflecting the imprisoning snow outside the windows. It glowed also with something more welcome, a large wood fire. The logs stacked by the grate had a pleasantly seasonable aspect, and the quiet peace of the hall was a comforting contrast to the wild white whirligig from which they had just escaped. The only thing absent to complete the welcome was their host.

But in his absence a large picture on the wall above the fireplace seemed to be doing the honours. It was an oil painting, in a heavy gilt frame, of an erect old man, whose eyes appeared to be watching them with a challenging cynical light. His eyes and his erect figure were not the only notable things about him. He possessed, for a man of his years, a remarkably fine head of black hair.

Other paintings were on the walls and climbed beside a curving staircase, but the uninvited guests were only conscious of the painting of the old man because of the subject's dominating presence.

David, after his first hurried glance, walked quickly to a couch near the fire and gently deposited his burden upon it. Jessie was just beginning to stir, but the comfort of the couch and the warmth of the fire seemed to delay the return to consciousness through a new, effort-combatting repose. He watched her for a moment or two, while the others stood about uncertainly.

"I suppose this is all right?" said the clerk, breaking the silence.

"It's got to be," answered Lydia. "I'm going to look in the rooms."

"Yes, there must be *somebody*," remarked David, glancing at the fire. "Try the kitchen. Perhaps they're hard of hearing."

Lydia vanished towards the back of the hall. In a minute she had returned, looking rather puzzled.

"No one," she reported. "But a kettle's boiling."

"Then somebody *must* be about," replied David.

"Certainly, but where about? There's a teapot on the kitchen table waiting to be filled, and a thingummy full of tea beside it. And the larder's stocked with provisions."

"You've been busy!"

"I'm going to continue being busy!"

She knocked on a door to the right of the hall. Receiving no response, she opened it cautiously and poked her head in.

"Jolly nice dining-room," she said. "Oak beams. And another fire going."

As she closed the door the clerk, struggling with an inferiority complex, decided to make himself useful. He darted to another door on the opposite side of the hall, and in his eagerness opened it without knocking. Fortunately for him this room was empty, also, but he received a surprise.

"I say! This is a drawing-room," he exclaimed, "and tea's laid!"

He became acutely conscious of Lydia's head peering over his shoulder and almost touching it. Accustomed to a dull, uneventful life, he was finding it difficult to keep steady amid his present emotions. The emotions were many and varied, including fear of illness, anxiety as to legal rights, and a nasty chilliness which might be due to the illness he feared or to a less definable cause.... This house, for all its fires, rather gave one the creeps ... But his dominant emotion at this particular instant was produced by the head that almost touched his shoulder.

"Funny!" said the owner of the head. "Tea all dressed up and nowhere to go! I say, David, what do you make of it?"

David turned from the couch.

"There's still upstairs," he replied. "I'll tackle that, if you'll stand by here."

"Wait a moment!" exclaimed Lydia.

"Why?"

"I don't know. Yes, I do. What I meant was, be careful."

"That doesn't explain anything."

"Nothing explains anything! If it were a fine day it might be quite natural to run out of a house for a few moments while a kettle's boiling, but in this weather—can you explain *that*? Where have they gone? Not to post a letter *or* to cut a lettuce! Why don't they come back? I didn't tell you, the kettle wasn't boiling in a nice quiet respectable manner, it was boiling over. Oh, and there was a bread-knife on the floor."

David looked at his sister rather hard.

"Are you getting morbid?" he inquired.

"No, darling," she retorted. "Just immensely interested!"

Then David went upstairs. While they heard him moving about Lydia walked to the couch and developed a practical streak.

"You know, we ought to do something about this," she said.

"What about dashing cold water into her face?" suggested the clerk. "I think that's what they do."

"A whiff of smelling-salts under her nose might be better," she answered. "I've got some in my bag. Where is my bag? Oh, here!" As she turned to it, she asked, "By the way, what's your name? Ours is Carrington."

"Mine's Thomson," replied the clerk. "Without a 'p.'"

He always mentioned that, believing it improved it.

"Well, Mr. Thomson without a p—by the way, you don't look too blooming yourself!—would you mind facing the kitchen and bringing a little cold water and a towel? Perhaps we might try your method before mine. Only we won't *dash* it at her, we'll just—No, whoa! Wait a moment!"

As she bent down the unconscious form fluttered, and suddenly Jessie opened her eyes.

"Take it easy," said Lydia, laying her hand gently on Jessie's shoulder and restraining a movement to rise. "Everything's all right, and we've plenty of time."

Jessie stared back at her muzzily, closed her eyes again, and opened them again.

"Did I go off?" she murmured.

"Right off," answered Lydia. "And then we found this house."

"But how——?"

"My brother carried you. I wouldn't talk for a bit."

"No, it was my foot——"

"Your foot?" Lydia stooped and examined it.

Then she turned to Thomson. "Yes, get some water, please, but hot, not cold. No, both. There's hot water in the kettle, and damn the tea!"

As she spoke, David came down the stairs. He shook his head in response to her quick, inquiring glance.

"Nobody?" she asked.

"Not a soul," he answered.

She glanced at him again, reading something in his tone. "He's more worried since he came down than he was when he went up," she decided. But his expression brightened as he saw Jessie.

"Oh, splendid!" he exclaimed. "How are you feeling?"

Jessie turned her head rather feebly, with a little smile.

"Just a bit funny, but quite all right," she replied.

"Yes, you told me you were all right last time," he smiled back. "I hope it's true this time."

"No, not this time, either," interposed Lydia. "She's twisted her ankle. Hurry up, Mr. Thomson. And, look here, don't damn the tea, after all, make it!"

With a ridiculous sensation that he was being heroic, Thomson found his way into the kitchen. So far, he had to admit, he had not done much. He had neither suggested this expedition nor led it. When the attractive blonde had fallen into the ditch he had not been the one to lug her out or to carry her to the house. True, he had been the first to strike the house. He had nearly struck it in the literal sense. But inside the house he had merely stood about and opened one door.

Now, however, his imagination became abruptly alive, spurring him to translate it into reality. Often, in his imagination, he came upon a lady aviator who had had a crash, and after lifting her gently from the wreckage, he carried her to a small empty cottage, made her tea, and married her. It was the tea touch here that recalled him to his pedestal. *He* was not the kind of man who rushed quickly and egotistically into the limelight—like, perhaps, Lydia Carrington's brother.... Nice chap, the brother, but just a bit too fond of his own voice.... No, Robert Thomson was one of those quiet, modest, dependable fellows, who gradually impressed themselves on a company—on such a girl, say, as Lydia Carrington—through sterling qualities. Your David Carringtons searched upper floors looking for people they knew they would not find, but your Robert Thomsons went into the kitchen and made the needed cup of tea ... and picked up the bread-knife from the floor....

At least—did they?

On the point of picking up the bread-knife, Thomson suddenly paused. A new aspect of himself had come to him daringly, startlingly, assisted by his rising temperature. He was no longer merely the quiet, dependable fellow who could make a cup of tea and keep the boat steady while others rushed about. Behind his unassuming manner lurked the detective brain, working silently and unsuspected!

This bread-knife, for instance. Just a knife on a floor, eh? Perhaps! On the other hand, perhaps not! The house was empty, but *somebody* had recently been in this kitchen; that was obvious from the boiling kettle; and if the somebody did not come back—and so far nobody had—there would be a reason for it. Maybe a dark, threatening reason, forming not only an immediate personal menace to the people within these walls, but a matter of wider interest to the public prosecutor.

Therefore, decided Thomson, any fingerprints on the bread-knife must not be erased. If you lifted the bread-knife at all, it must be lifted with a handkerchief, and before doing so you must note the exact position of the bread-knife, the direction in which it is pointing, the side which has the sharp edge ... and whether anything is on the sharp edge....

He became conscious of some one in the kitchen doorway behind him. He leapt round.

"Hurry up, old chap," said David. "We're still waiting for that water."

"Eh? Yes! I'm just getting it," exclaimed Thomson, jerked momentarily off his pedestal. "I—I was having a look at that knife."

David glanced at him curiously, and then at the knife.

"What about the knife?" he asked.

"Nothing," answered Thomson.

David crossed to the kettle, found a pan, and poured some water into it.

"I'll take this in," he said, "and you can get on with the tea."

Humiliation revived the clerk.

"They want some cold, too," he murmured, and rushed to a tap.

While Thomson filled a pail, David found a cloth and a sponge, and added them to his pan. Then he took the pail from Thomson and prepared to return. At the door, however, he paused.

"I wouldn't touch that knife," he said.

"I wasn't going to," retorted Thomson.

"Why not?" asked David. "Have *you* found anything?"

"No. What do you mean?"

"I see. Just wise precaution. Well, you're right. I *did* find something while I was ferreting about upstairs."

"What?"

"A locked door. Of course, it mightn't mean anything, only when I knocked I couldn't get any reply."

"People often lock doors when they go away," replied Thomson.

"Yes, but they don't leave other people behind the doors," answered David. He almost laughed at the clerk's startled expression. "Don't worry, the noise I heard might have been a mouse. By the way, when you come in with the tea don't mention our mouse. Let the tea do its work."

Lydia had removed Jessie's stocking when David returned with the water.

"Have you two men been playing bridge?" she inquired. "I thought you were never coming!"

"Sorry," said David. "I say, that foot looks swollen!"

"It is swollen," came the rejoinder. "What's the betting we all spend Christmas here."

"Oh, but I'll be all right!" exclaimed Jessie. "Anyhow, you wouldn't have to stay here for me!"

"You don't really think we'd all troop off and leave you here alone, do you?" asked Lydia. "But I wasn't only thinking of that. Look out of the window!"

The snow was falling as steadily as ever.

"Well, we're not such a bad party," said David, "if the worst comes to the worst—and the larder's full. I'm rather worried about old Mr. What's-his-name, though," he added. "I hope he found his way to somewhere."

He turned towards the stairs.

"Where are you going?" demanded Lydia.

"If you don't need me for the operation, I thought I'd just have another look round upstairs. After all, it *would* be rather nice if we could find somebody to ask us to tea."

"Well, trot along. We don't need you. But we're having tea whether we're asked or not!"

A sneeze exploded in the kitchen.

"Cook's catching cold," murmured Lydia. "I thought he looked a little green."

David went up the staircase for the second time. He glanced at the picture over the fireplace as he started, and the subject's bright, cynical eyes seemed to be following him.

The house was long and low, and there were only two main floors, but a narrow upper staircase ascended to what was apparently an attic, and it was the attic door that had been locked. The sounds he had heard on his first visit might conceivably have been due to a rodent as he had suggested, but he was not satisfied with that explanation.

The upper staircase was uncarpeted. Several of the stairs creaked. The one before the top was loose, and he stepped gingerly over it. Reaching the small square landing with its single door, he knocked.

As before, no one replied. But on the first occasion sounds had immediately followed his knocking. Now he heard none.

"This room's a nuisance," he thought. "Well, now I'm going to become one myself!"

He grasped the handle, turned and shook it. To his surprise he found the door was no longer locked. Shoving it open, he stared into a bare and empty room.

CHAPTER IV

TEA FOR SIX

WHEN David descended to the hall he walked into a fresh surprise. Mr. Edward Maltby, of the Royal Psychical Society, was standing in the doorway looking like a venerable snowman, while behind him was a second snowman less venerable. The second snowman was considerably bulkier than the first, and although David could see little of his face from where he stood at the foot of the stairs, what he saw did not create a favourable impression. He received a disconcerting sensation that a rather pleasant little party was being broken up.

Mr. Maltby, on the other hand, seemed momentarily unaware that any little party existed beyond his own. His eyes were rivetted on the picture above the fireplace, and his interest—thoroughly unreasonable at this instant—seemed to add to the portrait's queer significance. For several seconds after David's appearance no word was spoken. Then the old man lowered his eyes, and smiled.

"So you tried it, too, eh?" he said. "I hope your host has room for two more."

"We haven't got a host," replied Lydia. "At least, we can't find him."

"Really?" Mr. Maltby looked thoughtful. "Then how did you get in?"

"The same way that you did. The front door wasn't locked."

"I see." He turned to the man behind him. "Well, do we follow their example?"

"I dunno," answered the man. "P'r'aps we ought to move on."

"The suggestion is excellent but, like many excellent suggestions, impossible," retorted Mr. Maltby.

He entered the hall as he spoke. The man behind him hesitated, then entered after him. Mr. Maltby stepped back and closed the door.

"I am sorry to see you have had an accident," he said to Jessie. "I hope it was not a bad one."

"No, just my foot, I fell down," exclaimed Jessie. "It's a funny situation, I don't know what we'll all say when they come home."

"Perhaps they won't come home," remarked the old man.

"What makes you think that?" demanded Lydia.

"Did I say I thought it? Yet one might think it—in this weather—if they have been here at all to-day."

"We told you the door wasn't locked," David reminded him.

"So you did," nodded Mr. Maltby, and turned to the door. "A pity it is not a Yale lock."

"Why a pity?" asked Lydia. "If it had been a Yale lock we couldn't have got in."

"You mean we mightn't have got in," Mr. Maltby corrected her. "I agree that would have been a pity. And it is also a pity to let melted snow drip upon somebody else's carpet." He removed his coat and placed it carefully over the back of a chair. "But a Yale lock can be fixed open with a catch. This one might have been fixed. Then we should have had stronger evidence that the door had been deliberately left as we found it. Still, one sometimes, through careless oversight, forgets such things, or even to lock a door with an ordinary key, such as the one we have here."

"Your idea being," interposed David, "that the family might have left some while ago, and forgotten to lock up and to take the key with them?"

"But we have a fire to confound the idea," mused the old man.

"We have more than that, sir. We have a kettle boiling, and tea laid in the drawing-room——"

"And a bread-knife on the floor!" added Thomson, galvanically.

The old man regarded Thomson fixedly for a moment or two, and the clerk wished, without exactly knowing why, that he had not spoken. Then Mr. Maltby looked at each of the others in turn, including his massive, common companion—whose commonness had been proved by the one contribution he had so far made to the conversation—and ending up with the portrait over the mantelpiece.

"All this is very interesting," he commented. "Yes, extremely interesting. Including that picture. A remarkable old fellow. Yet not so very old, eh? How old? Sixty? A pleasant age, sixty. My own."

David fought a feeling of annoyance. Mr. Maltby, though a last-comer, had assumed a subtle command of the situation, and there was no reason that David could see, apart from the question of his sixty years, why he should do so. He had not merely changed the pleasant family atmosphere by emphasising the sinisterness of the place, an atmosphere which David had hoped to live down, but he was setting his own tone and his own tempo. "Why are we all hanging on his words like this?" David fretted. "He seems a decent old chap, but I don't like the way he seems to be wiping the rest of us off the slate! And I don't like that other fellow, either!"

"Something disturbs you?" queried Mr. Maltby.

David started.

"A lot disturbs me," he retorted, quickly concealing the real momentary cause. "I think we're all disturbed. Quite apart from the odd situation we're in, we've all got destinations to go to, and how are we going to them? How are we going to get away from here at all?"

"From my experiences in the last ten minutes," answered Mr. Maltby, "I am perfectly convinced that for awhile there will be no possible method of getting away from here at all. Therefore, let us be grateful that Fate has at least deposited us under a roof. And a roof beneath which there appear to be many comforts. A fire——"

"Several fires," interrupted Lydia.

"Indeed? The odd situation grows more and more intriguing. Several fires. And tea laid, too. If no one returns in, say, the course of the next three months, we might perhaps——?"

"We're jolly well going to perhaps!" smiled Lydia. "Tea's made, and we were just about to have it!"

"So *that* was not really worrying you?" inquired the old man, turning to David again.

"Oh! What was?" returned David.

"It was my question. Surely, not the bread-knife? By the way, I do not see it on the floor."

"It was on the kitchen floor."

"Was?"

"It still is," interposed Thomson again, boldly trying once more to impress his negligible personality on the company. "We didn't touch it. We left it there."

"That was most surprisingly wise. I take it, you did not wish to destroy the murderer's fingerprints?"

Jessie gave a little gasp. The cockney made his second contribution to the conversation.

"Wot's the idea?" he demanded, frowning.

"Come, come! A bread-knife on the floor!" exclaimed Mr. Maltby, insisting on his cynical humour. "Would not that convict anybody?"

"Not unless you found the corpse," replied Thomson, making an effort to keep up with him.

"Don't disappoint me? Don't tell me you cannot supply the corpse? A bread-knife on a floor, a boiling kettle, tea laid, an unlocked front door—and no corpse! Well, well, I suppose we must be satisfied, so let us be grateful and have tea. I am sure we all need it, and if the absent host manages to fight his way back through the snow and finds us making free with his larder and his crockery, I will deal with him. If he does *not* return, then we can leave behind us the price of the damage, and a note of gratitude. Eh? Personally, though you may not realise it, I am shivering."

"Oh, you must be!" cried Jessie. "Do come near the fire! Yes, that's a splendid idea, we'll leave a note and pay for it, and then I should think it would be all right. I mean, if it were the other way round and this were our house, wouldn't we think so?"

"I'm sure we would," answered Lydia, jumping up. "Come on, let's bring it here! It's cosier than the drawing-room."

The tight atmosphere suddenly loosened. A small table was found in a corner of the hall and was placed before the fire; the tea things were transplanted from the drawing-room; and under the influence of the warm, comforting liquid and bread-and-butter—some had been cut, and more was added, but not with the bread-knife—their predicament assumed a happier aspect. Lydia, with one eye on Jessie, who was pluckily recovering faster than nature intended, had decided that there must be no more talk of corpses and fingerprints, and she kept the conversation lively with a racy account of their journey through the snow.

"Of course, we were all perfect idiots," she concluded, as she poured out second cups of tea, "and we're in a funny mess, but in my opinion we're luckier than we deserve, not excluding you, Mr. Maltby," she added admonishingly, "and so I vote we make the best of it!"

"Aren't we?" asked Jessie.

"We are," nodded Lydia, "and we're going on as we've begun! Nobody's going to spoil *my* Christmas!"

"Hear, hear!" murmured Thomson.

Watching two attractive women out of the corner of his eye, and comparing them with his usual company at meals—and with the company he was going to—he had no present complaints. In fact, provided his nervous system could stand it—of that he was not quite sure, for his head was aching badly, but the tea and the fire gave him optimism—he believed he might welcome the eventual unearthing of a corpse, so that he could impress new stirring qualities upon these Venuses. "In any case," he decided, with the deliberate daring of his fevered thoughts, "I'll think of them to-night." Yes, it should be a bigger aeroplane that crashed in his nocturnal fancies. An aeroplane for two. And a slightly larger cottage. Or what about a house-boat on the Broads? The aeroplane could crash near the house-boat, where he would have been spending a lonely holiday, studying birds, say, and he would bring them there, and give them his room, and sit heroically outside all night.... *Atchoo!*

"I say, you *are* getting a cold!" exclaimed Lydia. "What about another log? And adding twopence to the bill?"

David, squatting on a stool by the couch, carefully avoided Jessie's bandaged foot as he bent forward and added a fresh log to the fire. The bandaged foot was a few inches from his nose. With the annoyance of an independent nature, he was trying hard not to notice it.

"What about *your* story, sir?" he asked Mr. Maltby. "We've not heard that. How did *you* find this place?"

"Yes, you left before we did, didn't you?" said Jessie. "Do tell us what happened? We tried to catch you up, you know, but then the snow covered your footsteps; we really felt quite anxious about you!"

"Please don't tell me yours was a search party!" exclaimed the old man, "and that *I* have led you into this?"

"Oh, no! We'd have gone anyway. Wouldn't we?" She appealed to the others. "Don't you remember, we were all talking about it. I think I was the one to start it, wasn't it, or wasn't I, I've forgotten? And then you suddenly jumped up as if you'd seen some one, and we thought *we* did for a moment, and we said perhaps it was Charles the First! Oh!" She turned to the cockney. "Was it you?"

"Me? No!" exclaimed the common man. "I wasn't on that train!"

He spoke with startling vehemence. Mr. Maltby broke a short silence by remarking:

"I came upon our friend—upon Mr.——?"

He paused invitingly.

"Eh?" jerked the man.

"Some of us have exchanged names," said the old man. "Mine is Maltby. May we know yours?"

"Why not? Smith."

"Thank you. Now we shall know what to write on our Christmas cards. I came upon Mr. Smith just outside here. In fact, we almost fell into each other's arms. I did think at first that he might be the person I saw leaving the train, but apparently I was wrong. How did you get caught in this terrible weather, Mr. Smith?"

"Well, it ain't pertickerly interestin'," replied the cockney.

"But we are interested," insisted the old man.

"Well, I was jest walkin'," said Smith.

"Yes."

"From one place to another, and the snow come on, and I got caught, like yerselves."

"Where were you walking to?"

"Eh?"

"We were trying to find another station," said Jessie.

"That's right, so was I," answered Smith.

"Another?" murmured Mr. Maltby.

"Wotcher mean?" demanded Smith. "I can try and find a stashun if I want to, can't I, without arskin' nobody's permishun——"

"I apologise," interrupted Mr. Maltby. "I was merely wondering, since you weren't on our train, why you should be searching for *another* station——"

"I never said another! She did!" He jerked his head towards Jessie.

"I apologise again. Which station were you looking for?"

"Eh?"

"I wonder whether it was the same as ours."

"Wot was yours?"

"Hammersby," said Jessie.

"That's right, 'Ammersby," nodded Smith.

The old man frowned slightly.

"Strictly speaking, Hemmersby," he murmured.

The atmosphere was growing tight again. All at once Smith turned on Mr. Maltby and exclaimed:

"Well, now you've 'eard abart me, wot abart you? I told yer I 'adn't nothin' interestin' to say, but p'r'aps *you* 'ave?"

"Yes, I have," replied Mr. Maltby. "Quite interesting. When I left the train…"

Then he paused. His eyes wandered from Smith to Jessie, and from Jessie to Lydia.

"You know, I haven't had *my* second cup of tea," he said.

"You haven't passed your cup," answered Lydia. "Thank you. Yes? When you left the train?"

"I've changed my mind," he responded. "This isn't the moment for ghost stories."

"When is the moment?"

"Perhaps this evening, if we are still here, and if we are in the mood."

The cockney rose abruptly.

"Well, *I* won't be 'ere, and I ain't in the mood," he exclaimed. "So long, and thanks, miss, fer the tea."

He walked to the front door.

"Just a moment," Mr. Maltby called after him, "you've dropped your ticket." Smith paused, as he held it out. "Euston to Manchester."

"That ain't mine," growled the man.

He completed his way to the front door and pulled it open. Snow poured in on him from the choked dusk. Something else came in, too. The echo of a muffled shout.

"Hey! Help!"

The man darted out, with David after him.

CHAPTER V

NEWS FROM THE TRAIN

THE first thing David did on emerging from the front door was to pitch head first into a mound of snow. For a moment or two he nearly suffocated, while countless soft, icy pellets invaded his back as though he were being bombarded by silent salvos from heaven. Then he scrambled out, and strained ears choked with snow for a repetition of the shout. Already he had lost his sense of direction, for all he could see was a bewildering succession of snowflake close-ups, almost blinding vision.

During the forty-five minutes he had been in the house the weather had travelled from bad to worse. Snow rushed at him unbelievably from nowhere caking him with white. He would have retreated promptly saving for the knowledge that somewhere in this whirling maelstrom was a man in a worse plight; but how to find the man, if his despairing cry was not repeated, seemed a stark impossibility.

He made a guess, plunged forward, and sank waist-deep. Some one helped him out. It was Thomson, trembling and gasping. They stared at each other, their faces close. And, as they stared, the voice that had brought them from the warmth of the fire summoned them again.

"Help! Some one! My God!"

The voice sounded a long way off, but actually it was close. Stumbling towards it, Thomson suddenly went flat. The mound he had fallen over writhed. Two rose where one had just fallen.

The addition was the elderly bore.

He was hatless, blue, and frozen. He tried to speak, and failed. The snow that melted round his staring eyes had a suspicious resemblance to tears. The man who had pooh-poohed English snow was receiving more than his deserts.

"Come on!" shouted David, flinging an arm round him.

Clinging to each other grotesquely, they swerved round and began stumbling back. The bore went down twice, the second time bringing his rescuers with him. When they were once more on their feet, they found a vague feminine form before them.

"Go back, you idiot!" croaked David. "Which way?"

"Not the way you're going, idiot yourself!" retorted Lydia.

She directed them back. Inside the hall they sank down and gasped.

"Well, what about Dawson City now?" panted David.

The bore offered no reply. Even if he had been physically capable of speech, his bemused brain could not have directed his tongue. He lay in the large chair in which he had been deposited, his eyes fixed vacantly on the ceiling, his face a mess of melting snow. Not attractive at the best of times, he now presented a most unsavoury appearance, and was temporarily too distressed to worry about it.

"This house is becoming a hospital!" Lydia whispered to Mr. Maltby.

The old man did not hear her. He was gazing towards the closed front door. The wind was rising, sending doleful music round the house, and periodically rattling the windows as though trying to get in. Suddenly, unable to stand it, Lydia dived towards a lamp and lit it. The illumination glowed on a strange scene. Three exhausted men, recovering at various rates of progress, but none in a hurry; Jessie Noyes, with her bandaged foot, and struggling against a return of fear; Lydia herself, frowning and tense; and the old man still gazing at the closed door.

"What is it? Do you hear anything?" demanded Lydia.

"I hear a lot of things," answered Mr. Maltby. "But not our friend Smith."

"No, he's gone, and good riddance," said David.

"Very good riddance, if he's gone," replied Mr. Maltby. "We are to take it that he has succeeded where the rest of us would fail." He gave a little shrug, and turned to the latest addition in the arm-chair. "When you have got your wind back we would like your story, sir. Meanwhile, to save your inevitable questions, here is ours. We all got lost. We all came upon this house. Necessity drove us in, and necessity retains us here. And apparently there is no one in the house excepting ourselves."

"Then, how the devil did you get in?" the bore managed to gulp at last.

"The door was not locked."

The bore gazed round, and began to take notice.

"Making yourselves at home, aren't you?" he asked.

"Thoroughly," agreed the old man. "Will you have a cup of tea?"

"My God! Will I?" Lydia poured him out a cup. He swallowed it too quickly and choked. "I don't suppose anybody could rake up a towel?"

This time Thomson obliged, fetching one from the kitchen.

"And what time would you like your shaving-water in the morning?" inquired Lydia.

In the process of mopping his face, the bore paused and looked at her suspiciously.

"I'm glad you think it's a joke," he muttered.

"The thought, I'm sure, is entirely self-defensive," interposed David. "You remember, Tommy made jokes in the trenches. Or—er—don't you remember?"

"I expect I remember better than you do, young man," retorted the bore, showing definite signs of recovery through the tea and the towel. He did not mention that his speciality during the war had been the making of munitions a long way from the sound of them. "But I am afraid my sense of humour isn't any too bright at the moment. I've been through a hell of a time."

He glanced at Jessie, as the only possible source of sympathy. Nice little thing, that blonde ... nice to get to know....

"Yes, will you tell us about the time?" asked Mr. Maltby. "We are curious to know why you left the train."

"*You* left it," answered the bore.

"And we were not thought highly of for doing so," remarked David. "I seem to remember an uncomplimentary observation."

"Are you trying to pick a quarrel, young man?"

"If you continue to call me 'young man,' I shall certainly pick a quarrel. Please remember that we've been through the hell of a time, too, and had the hell of a time lugging you out of a snowdrift."

"All right, all right, I apologise," grunted the bore. "We've all been through the hell of a time. And, if you want the truth, I left the train to escape another hell of a time."

"What, did the train get on fire?"

"It did not."

"What happened?"

"Perhaps I could tell you if I wasn't interrupted every other word."

"Sorry."

"Don't mention." He turned to Mr. Maltby. "Did you happen to see into the compartment next to ours, by any chance?"

"Which one?" inquired Mr. Maltby. "There were two. The one you were sitting back to?"

"Yes! How did you guess?"

"You wouldn't understand if I told you. No, I didn't see into it."

"Did any of the rest of you?"

They shook their heads.

"Ah! Well, you were spared something. At least—well, that depends on—on the time it——"

He stopped, and glanced again at Jessie. Her wide blue eyes were apprehensive.

"Wonder if I'd better go on," he muttered.

"I think you had," replied the old man. "If it is self-defensive to joke, it is also self-defensive to get used to shocks. The shock you are about to give us is unlikely to be our last."

"Oh, you know I'm going to give you a shock, then?"

"There is nothing occult in my perception of that."

"Perhaps you know what the shock is?" exclaimed the bore, stiffening suddenly.

"My dear sir," remonstrated Mr. Maltby, "do not look at me as though I were a murderer! *I* did not kill the person in the next compartment."

The bore became limp again as Jessie stifled a little shriek. He flopped back in his chair, and gave another mop to his face with the towel.

"Who—who told you—any one had been killed?" he gasped.

"You did," answered Mr. Maltby smoothly. "Emotions very highly developed frequently render words unnecessary. They progress along an ever-narrowing path, until at their peak they cease to be personal and achieve a universal aspect. We in this room merely appear to be different from each other when engaged on small concerns, but when we are fundamentally affected—with horror, love, excessive pain, excessive bliss—we are all the same."

"What the devil are you talking about?" muttered the bore.

"Homicide," replied Mr. Maltby. "Who is this person who has been killed?"

"Oh, you don't know *that*?"

"I would not ask if I did."

"Well, I don't know either. I mean, just some fellow or other. The guard found him. As a matter of fact I was out in the corridor when he came along—the guard—and I asked him a question, but he didn't answer. When I repeated it, he still didn't answer, and I found him staring into the compartment, so I joined him, and there was this man, lying on the ground—dead."

"Look here, hadn't we better have the rest of this later?" interrupted Lydia, glancing at Jessie, whose eyes were dilating.

But Jessie herself protested against a postponement.

"Why does everybody think I can't stand anything?" she demanded. "It's only my foot that keeps on twinging! Please go on!"

"I don't know that there's much more to go on about," answered the bore. "He was dead, and you can't bring a dead man to life again."

"Did you find out how he had been killed?" inquired Mr. Maltby.

"No."

"Have you any theory?"

"Is this an inquest?"

"Were there any signs of a struggle?"

"I don't know! I'm not a detective!"

"Detectives are not the only people with opinions. What did the guard think? Or do? Or say? I don't suppose you both stood there and played 'Buzz'?"

"Look here, I want to forget it!" retorted the bore. "Can't you see, I'm nearly dead myself? How do I know what the guard thought? All I know is that we soon had a crowd round us, and—and that while they were all staring and gaping, it seemed to *me* we wanted a policeman."

His tone took on a little flourish of triumph, as though he had suddenly justified himself in a company of doubters.

"I see," nodded the old man. "And that's why you left the train."

"That's it."

"While we sought a railway station, you sought a police station."

"Couldn't put it more neatly myself."

"Only you mentioned the word 'escape.'"

"Eh?"

"'I left the train to escape another hell of a time.' That was your expression."

"What are you getting at?" exclaimed the bore.

"I don't know that I am 'getting at' anything," replied Mr. Maltby, rather acidly, "but I suggest that, when you are telling a story of some importance you choose your words a little more carefully. Whether you actually left the train to assist the situation or to escape from it probably makes only a spiritual difference, for we may assume the material result would have been the same in either case, but in judging a man his point of view is more important than his action. Your own action, sir, unless the guard asked you to go for the police, or unless there is some vital factor of which we have not been informed, seems to have been definitely idiotic."

The bore glared.

"If you mean that it was idiotic to face this damned weather——!" he began.

"No, I did not mean that," interrupted Mr. Maltby. "I meant that a man in the next compartment is found dead, and you promptly leave the train."

"Come to that, we all left the train," said David.

"Thank you," muttered the bore. "So we all had a hand in it and *that's* settled!" He jumped up from his chair nervily, and then sat down again. "Look here, I feel dizzy. I've been nearly buried alive! If I'm not in for pneumonia, my name's not Hopkins!"

Thomson sneezed.

"Hallo, some one else getting pneumonia?" queried Hopkins.

"I should think we'll all get pneumonia," added Lydia. "Isn't that what inevitably happens when cold clothes dry on a numb body? I feel like hot ice!"

"So do I!" murmured Jessie.

"I'm sure you do. David, do you think you could carry her again? Upstairs, this time. And perhaps you could manage our suitcases, Mr. Thomson without a p. I don't care what anybody says, we're going to find a nice warm bedroom, and we're going to get properly rubbed down and dry!"

CHAPTER VI

SNEEZES OBLIGATO

A few minutes later David descended the stairs and found Mr. Edward Maltby alone in the lounge-hall.

Lydia's suggestion to make use of a bedroom had been seized on by Mr. Hopkins, who had declared that if the ladies were going to get dry there was no reason why *he* shouldn't, and who had followed them up. Then he had added to the unpopularity of his move by waiting to see which room David carried Jessie into, and promptly commandeering the room adjoining. Meanwhile Thomson, anxious to earn good marks, was sneezing and washing up in the kitchen.

"Aren't *you* afraid of pneumonia, sir?" David asked Mr. Maltby.

"I have more important things to think about than pneumonia," answered the old man.

"Pneumonia can be quite important."

"Yes, yes, but less important at my age than at yours. Some people think I have lived much too long already. Mr. Hopkins, for instance. Fortunately, you and your sister seem to be bearing up pretty well."

"Oh, we're all right."

"That is lucky. Our somewhat odd party needs a few able-bodied members to look after the rest. Our friend Mr. Thomson is sneezing his head off. Not that the absence of his head would make much material difference to his utility——"

"Come, sir, he *is* washing up!" interposed David with a grin. "As a matter of fact, I think I ought to go and help him."

"You will disappoint him if you do," retorted Mr. Maltby. "Mr. Thomson is one of those sensitive young men who need so much help that they insist on none. He is, as you say, washing up, and from sundry sounds I have heard between sneezes he is also breaking up. I imagine we shall have to include two cups and a saucer in the account for damages. I also imagine that, before midnight, our Mr. Thomson will be running a very high temperature. *He* is the one who ought to be in bed."

"He certainly looks a bit glassy," nodded David.

"So does the lady you have just carried upstairs. What is her name?"

"Jessie Noyes."

"Jessie Noyes. Well, she probably has a temperature, too. I am less certain about the last victim, Mr. Hopkins. My estimation of that individual is that he will develop a temperature if he wants to, but not otherwise. I undoubtedly have a temperature. Young man—I beg your pardon, you do not like being called young man."

"By Mr. Hopkins," qualified David.

"Thank you," smiled Mr. Maltby. "Personally, I should like to be called a young man by anybody. Still, I will avoid the phrase, in case you retaliate by calling me old man."

"My name is David Carrington."

"Well, Mr. Carrington, we have met in a most extraordinary situation, and it is this extraordinary situation that is causing me to pay no attention to my temperature. I am sorry to have missed Charles the First, but, do you know, I find that old chap up on the wall there equally interesting? In fact, I find this entire house interesting, though so far I have seen little of it—there goes another sneeze, and another cup—yes, and I am quite ready to contract pneumonia or any other physical complaint to discover its secret."

"Secret?" repeated David.

"You do not agree with me that it has a secret?" inquired Mr. Maltby.

"You mean, everybody being out, and the fires going?"

"Is that all?"

"No. The bread-knife on the floor."

"The bread-knife on the floor. Most important, that!... Yet, of course, it may be.... And that is all?"

David frowned.

"You know, sir," he said, "I think you and I might get on quite well if you'd be a bit more explicit."

"I have the same idea, Mr. Carrington," answered Mr. Maltby. "But I can only be explicit on one condition."

"What is it?"

"That you do not pass on what I tell you without my permission."

David hesitated. "I don't like giving blind promises," he said.

"I don't like exacting them," replied Mr. Maltby. "You are under no obligation to give this one."

"Only I won't hear what you've got to tell me if I don't?" The old man shook his head. "All right, I agree. No, wait a moment. Why am I privileged?"

"Because I may need some help before we leave this place. I may need some one to talk to—to think aloud to. You seem to me the best person for that office."

"Thanks. Well, sir, it's a bargain."

Mr. Maltby walked slowly round the hall. In his little tour he opened doors, looked up the stairs, and returned to the fire. Then he said:

"You have just heard about a tragedy on the train."

"We all heard about that," answered David.

"A bad tragedy. One that is going to affect us uncomfortably. But the tragedy on the train is not the only tragedy. Oh, no." He turned his head and glanced at the picture over the mantelpiece. The figure of paint appeared to be listening to the figure of flesh and blood. "There is another tragedy, and it may be that this other tragedy is going to affect us even more uncomfortably. You see, the horror on the train, great though it may turn out to be—as yet I know little about it—will not compare, I am certain, with the horror that exists here, *in this house*. Tell me, Mr. Carrington, am I just spinning melodramatic words to you, or do you feel the horror in this house?"

"I—I'm not sure," replied David unconvincingly.

"I am to accept that?"

"No."

"Then try again."

"Yes, I do feel it."

"I knew you did," answered Mr. Maltby. "We all feel it, but not in the same degree, or in the same way. Perhaps there is one exception at the moment. Mr. Hopkins. So far he has felt little beyond his own misery. But he will feel it, too, in due course, for all his pooh-pooh's. It would not surprise me at all if he is the first to crumble. . . . Your mind is rebelling against all this," the old man challenged suddenly. "You are saying to yourself, 'Oh, nonsense! This is just nerves! I am being

influenced by that silly spook-spouting old idiot Mr. Maltby.'
Let us examine that theory, then, to dismiss it. Did you begin
to feel something strange about this house after I arrived, or
before?"

"Before," admitted David.

"Then I cannot be responsible."

"It wouldn't seem so."

"When did you first feel it?"

"I suppose, pretty well as soon as I entered."

"Were your sensations general, or did any particular thing
strike you? We will exclude such items as bread-knives."

"Yes, one thing did strike me."

"What?"

"It doesn't seem any good telling you, since you appear to
know everything in advance."

"Of all there is to know, I know very little in advance. What
struck you?"

"Well, that picture over the fireplace."

"In what way did it strike you?"

"I don't know. Sorry if that's not satisfactory."

"Shall I put a suggestion into your head?"

"Please do."

"Did it strike you that the old fellow in the picture was
watching you? Listening to you?"

"But, of course, that was ridiculous!"

"Absolute nonsense. Well, what else struck you? You were
coming down the stairs as I arrived. I caught a glimpse of your
face. You were not very happy."

"I'd had a bit of a shock."

"Yes?"

"When you saw me coming down those stairs I was returning from my second ascent of them. I'd been poking round a bit before, and the first time I'd found a door locked. Top room. It worried me, because I thought I heard sounds behind it, but I got no reply when I knocked."

"What sort of sounds?" inquired Mr. Maltby.

"Nothing very distinct. Somebody moving, that was the impression. And then silence."

"Did you form any conclusion?"

"I can't say that I did."

"Of course, you tried the keyhole?"

"The key was in it, on the other side."

"Well? That was the first time."

"Yes. And the second time——"

"No, wait a moment," interrupted Mr. Maltby. "Have you told me everything about the first time? How long were you there? Was the sound repeated? It is a good plan, I have always found, to know all there is to know at once, then one does not have to go back to it."

"I agree that's a good plan," responded David, finding some comfort in the old man's thoroughness, "only in this case it doesn't advance us any, as I've told you the lot."

"On the contrary, Mr. Carrington, you haven't answered my specific questions."

"So I haven't. I was there about half a minute, I should say, and the sound wasn't repeated. No, wait—as we're being so particular! I've told you things in the wrong order. I didn't hear any sound till I knocked. Then the quick, faint movement. Then the silence."

"Thank you. And now for the second time."

"Yes, the second time," said David. "The door wasn't locked the second time. I walked into the room, a sort of attic, and found it empty. That's what gave me my shock."

"Naturally," nodded Mr. Maltby. "Did you form any conclusion this time?"

"Only that—that whoever had been in the room had now left it, and—and was somewhere else in the house."

"Not necessarily."

"What do you mean?"

"The window looked closed, or it would have occurred to you."

"Oh, I see. Well, it *was* closed, so it *didn't* occur to me."

"You examined the window?"

"No. I didn't do that."

"I think, when you examine it, you will find that it is closed, but not fastened. It may not even be completely closed. You may find——"

"Look here," interposed David. "If the person got out of the window, why should he worry about the door?"

"He may have tried the door first, and then suddenly changed his mind to the window," retorted Mr. Maltby. "Obviously your question cannot be answered without some knowledge of the person—whom we merely assume to be male—and his mental attitude. We must search the house very thoroughly, to make sure that this person is not hiding anywhere else. My own theory, however, inclines to the window. By the way, what did you think of our friend Mr. Smith?"

"Smith? That chap who came in with you?" queried David.

"Perhaps you are right to query the name," observed Mr. Maltby, dryly. "But we must use Smith for lack of another."

"I didn't think much of him," said David. "Nor did you."

"I am sorry I did not conceal my antipathy. No, I did not think much of him. You know, of course, that he was on our train?"

"I rather deduced that."

"Yes, it was unfortunate for him that he dropped his ticket. Now, since Mr. Smith was on our train, and stoutly denied the fact, what do you suppose would be the reason?"

David did not reply at once. The only reason he could suppose was a very unpleasant one, and while he waited some one emerged from the kitchen into the back of the hall. Thomson had finished his rather disastrous operations at the sink.

His face was paler than ever, despite a little pink spot on either cheek. The pink accentuated the surrounding white. His eyes were watering.

"Well, here we are!" he exclaimed, with a sort of glazed attempt at cheerfulness.

He stood for a few moments on one foot, and then sat down rather awkwardly in the nearest chair. It was a very hard chair, with a seat and back of dark polished wood. He looked as uncomfortable as he felt.

"Nice of you to do all the work," said David.

Thomson's advent had cut across the conversation and temporarily ended it. He was like a bit of grit that had got into a smoothly running engine.

"No, not at all, not at all," he replied. "I like washing up. Well, you know what I mean. If it's got to be done."

The pink spots grew pinker. He didn't want anybody to think his soul was so small that the pleasure of washing up filled it.

On the other hand, he didn't want to imply that he had been a martyr. Funny how you could sometimes think of the right words, and at other times they seemed a mile off. Lots of things seemed a mile off to Thomson at this moment. In fact, almost everything but the fire, and that was too close.

"Is it getting warmer?" he asked.

Before anybody could answer him he began sneezing. It was his longest bout.

"Seven," he murmured, smiling mirthlessly. "That must be a record. Not really, of course. I remember one chap who sneezed sixteen times. Hay fever. *Atchoo!*"

As Thomson came up from his eighth sneeze, his eyes caught a glimpse of something blue. It was the blue of a dressing-gown. It gave him a strange sense of peace, though also an impulse to cry. Of course, he mustn't do that. That would finish him! ... Hot? Had he said it was hot?

Mr. Maltby and David glanced at each other, and then at Lydia on the stairs.

"That fellow's going to be ill, if he's not looked after," murmured Mr. Maltby.

"Shall I put *him* to bed, too?" asked Lydia.

"Eh? What? I'm all right!" gasped Thomson, as the room swam. "I just get them sometimes. Colds. They don't mean anything."

"I'll take responsibility for this," said Mr. Maltby. "Stick him between sheets somewhere!"

A few moments later Thomson found himself being led up the stairs by the Most Beautiful Girl in the World. She had hold of his arm.... She was close to him ... Oh, nonsense! ...

"The one thing it is useless to fight, Mr. Carrington," remarked Mr. Maltby, "is the inevitable. I think we were talking about Mr. Smith."

The front door was shoved open the next instant, and the subject of their conversation staggered in.

CHAPTER VII

THE RETURN OF SMITH

SMITH was not a pleasant-looking object. His coarse rough suit was saturated with melting and melted snow, and his hair—he had no hat—streaked wetly down his low, lined forehead. Apparently his lips were the only dry portion of his anatomy, for before he spoke his tongue came out to moisten them. The action revealed the fact that several of his teeth were missing.

"Well, 'ere we are again," he said hoarsely, after a silence. "Gawd, wot a night!"

"Weather beaten you?" inquired Mr. Maltby quietly.

"You've said it," answered the man. "Worse'n ever!"

"Then how about closing the door to keep it out?" suggested Mr. Maltby.

Smith turned and shut the door. Then he glanced at the fire, walked to it, and spread out his hands.

"What happened to you?" asked David, breaking another silence. "We thought you'd gone for good."

"So did I, but I was wrong," retorted Smith. "*You* try!"

"You evidently did."

"Wotcher mean?"

"I think Mr. Carrington means that you vanished rather abruptly," said Mr. Maltby.

"Corse I vanished," answered Smith. "Yer vanish as soon as yet git outside!"

"Did you hear the cry for help?"

"Eh? No. Yus. Wot was it?"

"You made no attempt to find out?"

"Now, look 'ere, guv'nor," exclaimed the man, frowning, "I 'ad enough o' that larst time! I ain't come back to answer a lot o' questions, like I was in a witness-box, I come back to git warm, sime as you. See?" He spread out his hands again, and then rubbed them. "'Oo was it wanted 'elp?"

"If you don't answer questions, there is no obligation for us to," responded Mr. Maltby. "Still, you may as well know. It was somebody from the train——"

"Eh?"

"We told you we'd come from a train."

"Yus, that's right. So yer did. And this was another one, eh? Wot was *is* trouble?"

"The same as yours."

"Wot's that?"

"The weather. He got buried in it, and had to be pulled out."

"Oh! Well, where is 'e? Yus, and where are the others? There was more 'ere larst time, wasn't there?"

"They're getting dry upstairs," David told him.

"Upstairs?" repeated Smith, and glanced towards the stairs. "Well, wot abart it? I could do with a bit o' dryin' meself."

He made a vague movement towards the staircase, but Mr. Maltby, who had been watching him closely, moved in his way with a smile.

"Ladies upstairs, men in the kitchen," he said. "You understand?" As Smith did not appear to, he went on, "The ladies need some privacy."

"If you see somethink you ain't supposed to, you can look the other way, carn't yer?" muttered the man.

"I can," responded Mr. Maltby, rather tartly, "but I believe, with the majority, it is not always as easy as it sounds." Then suddenly Mr. Maltby's attitude changed. He laughed genially, and patted Smith's sleeve. "If the Fates decide that you are to spend Christmas with us here, Mr. Smith, you will be very welcome, provided you realise the situation is an odd one, and that we must all show the team spirit. Perhaps I myself have not given you a very good lead. You have accused me, for instance, of asking too many questions. Put it down to—to the natural nerviness of an old man, eh? And let us make a fresh start with each other."

He held out his hand. Smith looked astonished, then accepted it without any obvious enthusiasm, and a few moments later he had shuffled into the kitchen.

"Policy, Mr. Carrington," murmured Mr. Maltby, almost apologetically. "Merely policy. Our friend Mr. Smith must be temporarily placated, since evidently Fate *is* planting him among us for Christmas."

"Christmas isn't till to-morrow," David pointed out.

"True, perhaps I am over-pessimistic," admitted Mr. Maltby. "But, however long Mr. Smith is with us, we do not want to make him feel too uneasy. The lion springs when it believes it is to be attacked."

"Then——?"

"Yes?"

David looked towards the kitchen.

"We don't attack Mr. Smith?"

"Not till we are sure the attack will succeed."

"Meanwhile, are we sure *he* won't attack?"

"I am quite sure he won't attack without a motive, which is why I am trying to remove the motive. That does not mean," he added, "that we shall cease to watch Mr. Smith. In fact, I am half inclined to allot you the task of doing so while I go up and have a look at that attic."

"Thanks frightfully!"

"Not at all. If Mr. Smith returns here before I do, keep him occupied, and be nice to him. Where exactly is the door you found locked?"

"Right at the top. There's only one."

The old man moved towards the stairs.

"You noticed, of course," he said, pausing, "Mr. Smith's anxiety to go upstairs? That did not escape you?"

"I also noticed your own anxiety not to let him go upstairs," answered David. "Did you think *he* was making for the attic?"

"I never think what I am certain of. He was undoubtedly making for the attic. It is even possible that the attic, as well as the weather, brought him back, though I am *not* certain of that. Mr. Smith has already been in the attic once, and it is merely on a matter of form that I shall compare, if I can, the fingerprints I find there with his own. Particularly those on the window-sill."

"You don't mean ——?" began David, and stopped abruptly.

"That you were not the first to enter this deserted house?" said Mr. Maltby. "That is exactly what I mean. Mr. Smith was the first. He was in the attic. He left via the window; in a minute I shall be in a position, I expect, to tell you how he did it. And then he re-entered the house with me. This, according to my calculation, is his third visit."

"Wait a moment!"

David glanced again towards the kitchen, then ran to the old man's side.

"Do you think Smith committed the murder on the train?" he asked, lowering his voice.

"What do *you* think?" countered Mr. Maltby.

"I think we ought to try and get the women out of here," said David.

"There is only one argument against that," answered Mr. Maltby. "Its utter impossibility. But Smith isn't our biggest trouble, Mr. Carrington. After all, he is flesh and blood; we can deal with Smith."

CHAPTER VIII

IN A FOUR-POSTER BED

"WELL, there's another of us in bed!" exclaimed Lydia. "Who's going to be the next?"

Jessie Noyes, in bed herself, looked up from her diary as Lydia re-entered the room. Jessie had only remembered the consolation of her diary a minute or two earlier, and had not got farther than "This is the rummiest day I have ever spent, not even counting that time the burglar got into my room and we ended up telling each other's fortunes," when Lydia interrupted her. Slipping the diary under her pillow, she answered:

"I hope it won't be *you*! How is Mr. Thomson?"

"Higher and higher," replied Lydia.

"Do you mean his temperature?"

"Yes. I'm afraid poor Mr. Thomson isn't going to spend a very comfortable Christmas."

She walked to the window, drew the curtain aside, and stared through diamond panes at the battle between black and white. The white was winning, though the black spread its dim shadows over the field of war.

"The snow's getting higher and higher, too," commented Lydia, suddenly replacing the curtain and turning round to the pleasanter picture of an oak-beamed room, with rafted ceiling and four-poster bed glowing in firelight. "We'll probably wake up to-morrow morning buried!"

"If we hadn't found this place, we mightn't have woken up at all!" added Jessie sagaciously.

"That's true! Thankful for small mercies. Only, it does seem queer. Because here's another 'if.'" She glanced at her little gold wrist-watch. "Yes, if our train hadn't given up the ghost, at about this moment David and I would have been entering a big house full of people and holly and mistletoe, with shops and buses and a cinema round the corner. And a large man with a prickly moustache would be crying, 'Hallo, Lyddie, got a kiss for Uncle Bill?'" She laughed. "Well, we can't supply the shops and the buses and the cinemas here, or the kiss for Uncle Bill, which quite privately doesn't worry me any, but we're going to have the decorations, that's a promise!"

"I don't see how."

"I'll find a way. As I said before, nobody's going to spoil *my* Christmas!"

Jessie smiled faintly. Lydia's robust enthusiasm was more warming than the fire.

"Of course, we mustn't forget this isn't our house," the chorus girl murmured.

"My dear, after the liberties we've already taken, decorations will be a detail! Anyhow, I don't know how *you* feel, but my own sense of what's right to do and what's wrong to do has become completely tangled up and demoralised! We seem to have got into a sort of—what? Current? And it's taking us where it likes, so why worry?" But it was the final flicker of worry that caused her to build up her defence. "Could we help the ridiculous snowdrift that stopped the train? No! Could we help losing our-selves? No——"

"We could have stayed in the train."

"That doesn't make it a crime to have left it! And then your accident, and the risk of pneumonia, and the stark staring necessity of getting tea inside us and towels outside us—we had to get dry, didn't we?—and Mr. Thomson's tem-perature, and the impossibility of going anywhere else, and nobody being here to say either 'Yes' or 'No' to reasonable requests. One thing I feel quite sure of, anyway. To move Mr. Thomson would be homicidal. I've even given him a hot-water bottle!"

"I suppose there's no way of getting a doctor?" asked Jessie.

"Not a hope," replied Lydia. "Even if there were a telephone, which there isn't, the doctor could never get here. I wonder how they're getting on downstairs? Do you mind if I leave you again for a few moments and pop below?"

"Of course not! I'm all right."

"Back soon."

By herself again, Jessie lay back on her pillow for awhile and stared at the canopy of faded pink above her. She had never lain in a four-poster bed before, and she found the sensation rather singular. At first it was pleasant. She felt herself sinking back into an easy, amiable past, where the fight for bread-and-butter—often so sordid a fight—did not exist. The snow dissolved with the years. Outside was sunny country; inside, slow movement, and ease.

Then, gradually, the ease departed, and a strange fear began to invade her. She put it down to natural oppressions—her slightly aching foot, the strain she had been through, worry about her lost chance of an engagement and the difficulty of finding another, and the grunting and occasional coughing of the objectionable man in the adjoining room. None of these causes, however, seemed to fit her new mood. It was a fear to which she could not adjust any coherent cause. It grew until it gave her a definite pain in her stomach. She sat up suddenly, in the grip of a nameless, apprehensive terror. She felt as though the walls and the bed-posts were pressing upon her....

"What's the matter with you?" she gasped, struggling to regain her normality. "*Aren't* you a little idiot?"

Her diary slipped from under the pillow and slid down the
sheet to her side. She seized it gratefully, comforted by its familiar aspect. Then she continued writing as though there had been
no interruption:

"Our train got snowed up and I and some others tried to walk
across country to another station, Hammersby, no Hemmersby,
well one or the other, but the snow was so bad that we got lost,
and then I fainted like a fool, twisting my foot, and a young man,
his name is David Carrington, very nice, carried me to the house
where we now are and may have to stay till the snow stops if it
ever will. It's funny because although no one is here the tea was
laid and the fires going. We had the tea, they all said it was all
right, but I don't know, though of course we needed it, and then
after some more turned up David C. carried me up to the room
where I now am, he's very strong, and now I am in bed, of course
he went, though I'm not undressed, and very comfortable."

She paused. She had written the last two words almost defi-
antly. She went on, to ease her conscience and propitiate the
Fates:

"Of course, it's a funny situation. One does worry a bit about
the shocks we'll all get if the family returns, though how could
they, and my foot still hurts, not very much. Then some of the
people here are rather trying. I don't mean Mr. Thomson, one's
rather sorry for him, he's in bed with a temperature (another)
(bed), and of course I don't mean the Carrington's, the brother
and sister, Lydia's very nice and David is one of those people you
can like at once without minding, the kind you can trust. Very
good-looking. But an old man (Mr. Maltby) gives one the creeps
rather, he's pyschic if that's the way to spell it, and there's another
man, common, but thank goodness he's gone. The one I hate
most, though, is Mr. Hopkins, I know the type. He's followed us

from the train with a horrible story about somebody being killed on it, and he's in the next room now, while I'm writing. I know he chose it on purpose because I'm in this one, and I'll bet he's had his eye at the keyhole of the door between. He wanted me to stay behind in the compartment with him, and when I think that if he'd had an engagement to offer me I might have stayed, loathing it, it makes you feel horrid. I wonder if I'll ever change, or if it's my fault if I don't? You've got to live. Even the burglar said that, I wonder what's happened to him, and if I really lost that brooch, or if he took it? Really, you try to trust people, but it doesn't seem sometimes as if you ever can, it almost makes you want to cry, only of course I expect I'm as bad as the——"

Her pencil stopped moving abruptly. The door had opened softly, and Mr. Hopkins was looking in.

"Oh, this is *your* room," he exclaimed, with unconvincing surprise.

"It looks like it, doesn't it?" she retorted, closing her diary sharply.

"I thought it was mine."

"Of course, don't trouble to apologise."

"I didn't."

"So I noticed. And as this *isn't* your room, you'd better go away again."

Mr. Hopkins frowned. He was in his shirtsleeves, and his thumbs were through his braces in the arm-holes of his waist-coat.

"No need to be cross!" He turned his head and glanced into the passage behind him. "This is a queer mess we're in, and we've got to pull together."

"Do you call it pulling together coming into my room, and not going out when I tell you to?" asked Jessie.

He shrugged his shoulders, made a movement to go, then altered his mind.

"Look here!" he said. His voice had an excited nerviness in it. He had lost the irritating assurance that had rendered him unbearable in the train; but he was no more bearable now. "We're in a *mess*! Do you know it? In a mess!"

"Yes, of course, I know it," she answered, "and if you're found here it'll be a worse mess!"

"Nobody's going to find me here! I'm not a fool, and I don't suppose you are! I read you as a smart girl who knows what's good but doesn't lose her head. Kind I like. Now, then, now, then," he added hastily, "don't pull that face! All I'm suggesting is that—that if we're going to be cooped up in this confounded asylum for a bit, well, a little friendliness wouldn't do either of us any harm, and might bring you a very nice Christmas present."

As he vanished Jessie was divided between indignation and a humiliating wonder as to what sort of a present a man like that would make; but she did not have long to dwell on either point, for Lydia returned almost immediately afterwards, and her return explained Mr. Hopkins's abrupt departure.

"If you're thinking of trying to get up," said Lydia, as she closed the door, "I wouldn't. You and Mr. Thomson are in the best places to be!"

"Why, what's happened?" asked Jessie anxiously.

"Mr. Smith has happened," answered Lydia. "He's happened back again. I didn't see him—he was in the kitchen—but my brother told me. He was alone in the hall."

"Where was Mr. Maltby?"

"Poking around upstairs somewhere."

"What for?"

Lydia shook her head angrily.

"My dear, you and I are what are popularly known as 'the women'—we're not to know things! David and I nearly had a row about it!"

"Do you mean he wouldn't say anything?"

"Well, he told me about Mr. Smith, but when I began asking questions he shut up like a clam. 'Everything's all right,' he kept on repeating, in that disgusting run-away-and-play voice. 'If everything's all right,' I said, 'why do you look as if everything's all wrong?' Have *you* got a brother?"

"No."

"You are thrice blessed. Oh, he did give me one other bit of cheering news, though. The snow outside the front door is half-way up."

"Gracious!"

"Yes, we're properly imprisoned. Thank God, the larder's full!"

"But we can't go on eating other people's food!" exclaimed Jessie.

"Miss Noyes," replied Lydia, "suppose this house belonged to you, and you returned to it after the world's worst snowstorm, would you rather find your larder empty or seven skeletons? If we are to go to prison for refusing to oblige the law and starve, we'll go to prison!"

"Yes, of course," murmured Jessie. Then suddenly she asked, "What happened to the bread-knife?"

"Bread-knife?"

"I just wondered whether it was left in the kitchen."

"I expect so. I'm sure I don't know. My dear, we won't get morbid!" She knew what had been in Jessie's mind. It was difficult not to dwell on Mr. Smith and the gruesome story Mr. Hopkins had brought from the train. To change the subject she went on, "Oh, I forgot! David sent you his love and hoped you were feeling better."

Jessie flushed at this pleasant fabrication.

A silence fell upon them. Lydia went to her suitcase and began examining the contents. Jessie watched her for a while, then asked:

"What are you doing?"

"Seeing what presents I've salved from the train."

"You won't need them here."

"I may. Christmas has got to be Christmas, wherever you spend it. Would you like a dear little white bunny or a golliwog?"

Jessie laughed. Without the Carrington's, she felt the situation would have been unbearable.

The door of the adjoining room opened and closed. Jessie stopped laughing, and Lydia raised her head, catching sight of Jessie's face in the dressing-table mirror.

"There goes our bore," she said. "You don't like him any more than I do, do you?"

Jessie hesitated for an instant. Her virtues, like her vices, were simple. One of the virtues was that she hated talking ill of people. She had had plenty of opportunities.

"We can't help being what we are," she replied.

"No, if a tiger eats you, it isn't really his fault," answered Lydia. "God gave him his appetite. He's going downstairs. Mr. Hopkins, not the tiger." She listened. "He has a heavy, distressed tread. Have you noticed how circumstances have changed him?"

"What do you mean?"

"You're the same. I'm the same. But people like Mr. Hopkins alter with the weather. They're up at top when things are going right, and down at the bottom when things are going wrong.

In the train, compared with Mr. Hopkins, we were all tiny little worms. Of course, things weren't going right in the train, but they hadn't reached this pass. Now he's becoming the worm. Yes, I think I'll give *him* the golliwog. Hallo, somebody else! Who is it this time? I hope Mr. Thomson hasn't become delirious!"

She ran to the door and opened it a crack.

"Maltby," she reported, closing it, "of the R.P.S. He's another rum one, though I rather like him. I wonder what he's been poking about upstairs for? Half a mind to do some poking myself."

"Don't!" exclaimed Jessie.

Lydia gave a little sigh.

"Perhaps you're right. But I'm wondering how long we can go on like this? Somehow everything seems so—I don't know—unsatisfactory."

"We're lucky to have found a roof."

"Oh, yes—that. Only it all might have been so different. Suppose, for instance, our party had been you and me and David and two or three others more like us. We'd have made a team. Had fun. But, as it is, we're all bits and pieces. We don't fit. Mr. Maltby thinks only of his psychic vibrations; Mr. Hopkins of his comfort; Mr. Smith, well, I don't know what he's thinking about, but I'm sure it isn't up our street; and poor Mr. Thomson ... what we need is pulling together, yes, and don't be too surprised, Miss Noyes, if you see me behaving astonishingly!" she exclaimed suddenly. "The one thing that can save us from causing each other nervous break-downs, if we're to be forced on each other for much longer, is a common object, and that common object is Christmas itself. If we can't leave this place, it's no good sitting about watching the front door. Yes, from this moment I'm going to work to make this the jolliest Christmas of our lives! You'll help me, won't you?"

"Yes! Of course!" replied Jessie rather breathlessly. "But what can I do?"

"You can just lie there and back me up. Help me to feel I'm not doing this all alone. Once I get a start David will join in, and it'll grow like a snowball. Only it won't grow on empty stomachs," she added. "What would you like for dinner? Dinner's at eight. Tomatoes and spaghetti?"

In the full tide of her enthusiasm, she ran from the room.

Jessie opened her diary again and wrote:

"——rest. But I'm sure I'm not as bad as Mr. Hopkins. Or as good as Lydia Carrington. I hope she won't be gone too long. Somehow, when she's not here, this room seems to get on top of me."

CHAPTER IX
STUDIES IN ETHICS

For a few minutes after Mr. Maltby left him for his tour to the attic, David sat and smoked. He had rather less fear than the average, although his courage had never been yet severely tested, and he was not worried personally that an alleged murderer was in an adjacent kitchen, trying at that moment perhaps to remove bloodstains! Smith might be homicidal, but he had shown no symptoms of insanity, and it was not likely that he would suddenly leap back from the kitchen and plunge the bread-knife in David's back. There were others, however, whose nerves might be more severely strained by the situation if they became fully alive to it, and Mr. Maltby's policy of endeavouring to keep a wild animal tame and unsuspecting was obviously sound.

Other matters, also, needed the soothing influence of tobacco smoke. David possessed a normal respect for property, and his ethical as well as his legal sense was troubled by the free use that was being made of the house. He imagined himself the owner, returning suddenly and plugging the uninvited guests with indignant questions. "What do you mean by coming into my house?" "The door wasn't locked, we had to get some shelter." "Well, why not somewhere else?" "There wasn't anywhere else. We were nearly frozen, and one of our party had had an accident." "Did that excuse you for drinking my tea?" "We needed it pretty badly; we had an idea you'd have offered it if you'd been here." "All right, let it go. But you're using the bedrooms!" "Yes, two." "Suppose I need them for myself, for my own party?" "In that case, of course, you must have them, and you can't turn out a girl with a damaged foot and a man with a high temperature. Do you suppose we'd have used them if there hadn't been real need? And do you suppose we'd have even used your towels and dried ourselves if we hadn't been up against it? Some of us might have got pneumonia!" "You've miscounted. *Three* bedrooms are being used." "I hold no brief for the third." "All right, *let* that go. But suppose I hadn't come back? Suppose I hadn't come home at all?" "We didn't think you would." "Why not?" "For the same reason that we're here—the weather." "But you knew I'd *been* here—I or somebody! Who laid the tea and put the kettle on and lit the fires?" "We had no idea." "Did you try to find out?" "Obviously." "How?" "We searched the house." "What about outside the house?" "Impossible." "Are you quite sure?" "Look!..."

Having reached this point in the imaginary conversation, he jumped up and went to the front door. Opening it, he showed the imaginary interrogator the banking snow in the porch. If he had intended to stagger the imaginary one with the sight, he forgot this in his own astonishment. The bank had mounted almost beyond belief and was now a glimmering white wall.

"I don't believe we could get out of this door now if we tried!" he said aloud. "So tell me this, old chap, how the devil did *you* get in?"

He closed the door, relieved by this further argument in his favour. They *couldn't* get away. Which, in its turn, meant that the owner of the house couldn't return and the imaginary cross-examination couldn't take place. For the first time in his life, David was realising the true meaning of the word, "snowbound."

"And, the situation being what it is," his mental defence continued as he returned to the fire, "are we to die of cold and starvation, when the means of staving off each is at hand? Is that humanly reasonable? Would a shipwrecked party thrown up on a desert island wait for legal permission to eat the cocoanuts?"

The legal aspect brought him suddenly to an entirely different question.

"What is the penalty for harbouring murderers, if any?"

He turned towards the kitchen. He listened to vague sounds. Then another sound caught his ear, and he turned to the staircase. Lydia was coming down for the unsatisfactory interview she described on her return to Jessie.

"Any news?" she asked, as she reached the bottom.

"Have *you*?" he parried.

"Dear brother, I asked first!" retorted Lydia. "Don't be irritating!"

"Well, I have one bit of news," he said. "Our friend Smith has returned——"

"What! That horrible man——"

"Shut up!" growled David. "He's in the kitchen."

"Oh, thanks for the warning," she answered, lowering her voice. "What's he doing in the kitchen?"

"Getting clean. So now run upstairs again, or he may come out and see you."

Lydia regarded her brother indignantly.

"Will he eat me if he sees me?" she demanded. "Really, David, you're being rather bright! Or is there something you haven't told me? I know he's a sort of suspect, but——"

"Well, if he's a sort of suspect, why not keep clear of him?" interrupted David. "Do go!"

"Where's Mr. Maltby?"

"Upstairs."

"What, is *he* getting to bed, too?"

"Of course not!"

"Then what's he doing?"

"I don't know."

"Try again?"

"Why should I know?"

"I don't know why you should, but I know you do. You'll go to heaven, David, you're such a rotten liar! What's Mr. Maltby doing upstairs, or am I too young to be told?"

David took a deep breath.

"Mr. Maltby is poking around upstairs, urged by an insatiable curiosity," he said. "You forget, he has the scientific mind."

"I didn't see him on the first floor."

"Then he must be on the second."

"That's the top floor, isn't it?"

"Lydia, does all this matter?"

"Not a bit, darling. I'm only trying to irritate you as much as you're irritating me, but I think I've taken on more than I can manage. I say, *aren't* we peace-and-goodwilly? So that's the lot, is it?"

"No, there's one thing more, if you want it," he replied. "The snow outside the door is higher than ever, and it's still coming down."

"Thought for the day. The more the snow comes down the more it comes up. Never mind, dear, we're all tired; perhaps we'll love each other next time. Kind regards to Mr. Smith."

As she ascended and disappeared, he turned again to the kitchen. At the same moment the door opened, and the man who called himself Smith took shape out of the shadows.

"Hallo; how are you getting on?" asked David.

"I've 'ad a wash," replied the man.

"Well, cleanliness is next to godliness," said David. "Feeling all right again?"

The man nodded. David found himself staring at his big rough hands.

"Where's the others?" inquired the man, after a little silence.

"They'll be down in a few moments," answered David. "Have a fag?"

"I don't mind if I do," grunted the man. "Upstairs, eh?"

David offered his case and struck a match. When the man's cigarette was gleaming between his thick lips he moved casually towards the staircase. David moved casually with him.

"What's all this abart?" exclaimed the man suddenly.

"What's all what about?" asked David innocently.

"Nothink!" muttered the man.

He sat down on the bottom stair and puffed for a while. David studied his face through his own tobacco smoke. The man had a pasty complexion, and although he had said he had washed, the statement was necessary to impress an otherwise doubtful fact. His eyes, surly beneath heavy black eyebrows, were too close together, and he had a boxer's nose. Probably he had helped to give somebody else a similar identity mark.

"Well, it might be worse'n it is, mightn't it?" he commented with a rather suspicious change of attitude.

"The weather mightn't," answered David.

"I mean in 'ere."

"Ah, in here, I agree."

"There's warm fires."

"One might even describe them as scorching."

"Wot?"

"I merely agreed with you again. Go on counting your blessings."

The man frowned, then smiled.

"Well, 'ere's another blessin'," he continued. "Plenty o' stuff in the bloody larder."

"I take it you have looked," murmured David.

"Yus, and I tike it I wasn't the fust!"

"You were not."

"Orl right, then! So nobody can't say wot I begun it. No, and when the bloke wot this 'ouse belongs to comes 'ome and finds there ain't so much in it as wot there was when 'e left, don't blime *me*!"

David looked thoughtful. A new aspect of this man's presence was beginning to dawn.

"Nobody's going to blame anybody, Mr. Smith," he said, "so long as the stuff we remove is strictly perishable."

"Wot's that?" jerked Smith. "Perishin'?"

David decided to apply a little test, in the centre of which was wrapped a warning.

"Listen, this is how I've worked it out," he replied. "As a matter of fact, I was working it out in here while you were removing—washing yourself in there." He nodded towards the kitchen. "I'm really no happier about all this than you are yourself——"

"Eh?"

"I mean, like you I can't help worrying about the food we've taken, and that we may have to go on taking——"

"Oh, we're goin' on, are we?"

"Well, if we're imprisoned here all night I expect we'll have to——"

"Imprisoned—orl night?"

"You know the weather as well as I do."

"That's a fack."

"So I don't have to tell you that we *may* have to stick here all night."

"That's right."

"In which case, as I was just saying, we shall wake up hungry, won't we?"

"Corse."

"So——"

"'Arf a mo."

"What?"

"S'pose when we wike up termorrer mornin' it's *still* snowin'?"

"Then it will be a real White Christmas, and we mustn't turn it black."

"Look 'ere!" exclaimed Smith, with nervy impatience. "Why carn't yer tork like an ordin'y bloke? If you've got anythink to say, say it and 'ave done with it!"

"I am longing to say it and have done with it," retorted David, "and I should have said it and had done with it years ago but for your continual interruptions! Perishable goods, to get back to our muttons——"

"Mutton?"

"Do you want me to hit you?"

"Try it on, guv'nor!"

"I should hate to try it on, but I may have to. Perishable goods are things to eat. If we are destined to have breakfast here, followed by lunch, tea, and Christmas dinner, we shall be forced to take more perishable goods, i.e., more things to eat. But we shall pay for them, and we shall *confine* our burgling to perishable goods, i.e., things to eat. We shall steal merely to live. And pay for what we steal."

"Well, that's orl right——"

"Quite all right. But it wouldn't be all right if—well, if I got interested in a book I happened to find here, and went away with the book in my pocket. The rest of you would probably jump on me. Get the idea?"

"'Oo'd go away with a book in 'is pocket?" answered Smith with a sudden grin.

"I was speaking of myself," responded David. "I'm quite sure you wouldn't."

"Corse I wouldn't!"

"There we are, then."

"If I went away with anythink in me pocket, it'd be the duchess's diamonds."

David smiled back.

"Then it's very lucky," he said, "there are no duchesses here. Hey, where are you going?"

For Smith had risen from the stair and thrown his cigarette away.

"Stretch me legs," replied the man.

"Not upstairs."

"Why not upstairs?"

"Well, you heard what Mr. Maltby said."

"That old bloke?"

"Yes."

"Is 'e me father?"

"It would probably be news to him."

"Then 'ere's some news fer you! We're orl 'ere without permishun and we're orl in the sime boat, and I ain't takin' orders from nobody! See?"

He swung round and begun to ascend.

But he stopped half-way up. The stout figure of Mr. Hopkins came round the bend of the stairs, to stop just as abruptly.

"Hallo! Who are *you*?" exclaimed Mr. Hopkins.

"Come to that, 'oo are you?" retorted Smith.

"No need to be impudent!" snapped Mr. Hopkins. "My name is Hopkins, sir! I suppose you're another off the train?"

"Well, you s'pose wrong! I ain't off the trine."

Mr. Hopkins shrugged, then suddenly looked at the man more closely.

"What's the idea?" he demanded. "Of course, you were on the train! I saw you!"

CHAPTER X

WOMAN DISPOSES

A DULL flush spread over the cockney's cheeks. The cheeks of Mr. Hopkins, on the other hand, became suddenly paler as he regarded a clenched fist uncomfortably close to his nose.

"I'm a liar, am I?" shouted the cockney.

"Now, then, there's no need to get so excited!" muttered Mr. Hopkins.

"No need ter git excited!" retorted Smith. "Corse, it wouldn't excite *you* if a bloke called you a liar? 'Ave another look at me!"

A faint perspiration glistened on Mr. Hopkins's forehead.

"Yes, I see I was mistaken," he said. "I have never seen you before in my life, and I sincerely hope I never see you again!"

"And that's a 'ope," growled Smith, "becose' ain't I snowed up 'ere sime as you, so you'll 'ave ter stick seein' me, see? Well, 'ow much longer are yer goin' ter stand there? Are you comin' dahn, or am I goin' up?"

Mr. Hopkins swallowed and stepped aside. The cockney brushed past him unceremoniously, deliberately barging him against the wall as he did so. It was significant of Mr. Hopkins's mood that he accepted the insult without protest.

"For all his bragging, Hopkins is a confounded coward!" thought David.

But the cockney's passage to the top of the stairs was still not free, for now there occurred a second block in the traffic, and Smith found Mr. Maltby in his path. Ready for a further altercation, Smith glared at the old man; but the old man merely smiled back.

"Going to have your little look round?" he inquired genially.

"'Oo's goin' ter stop me?" replied Smith.

"Why should any one stop you?" answered Mr. Maltby, making space for him. "I wish you a pleasant tour. But don't go into any room without knocking. The ladies are in one, and there is a sick man in another."

"Thanks fer the information."

"Not at all. It was given to you for their benefit, not for yours. Oh, but this *is* for your benefit—there is one more room I would not go into, if I were you."

"'Oo's in that one?"

Mr. Maltby hesitated for a moment, then responded, "I cannot say, but—some one."

"Wotcher mean?" demanded the cockney, pausing, while David and Mr. Hopkins stared.

"You will always find, Mr. Smith, that I mean exactly what I say; it is a time-saving method," returned the old man. "I am telling you that some one is in that room, and I do not know who it is."

"Oh! I see! Yer mean yer 'eard some 'un, and yer didn't go in?"

"I went in."

"I don't git yer."

"That does not surprise me."

"Wot did they say when yer went in?"

"They did not say anything."

"Oh! Then wot did *you* say?"

"I did not say anything, either."

"Yer jest looked at each other, and thort?"

"I certainly did considerable thinking. You see, if I had spoken to the—some one—I should have received no answer."

The voice of Mr. Hopkins came up sepulchrally from the bottom of the stairs.

"You—you don't mean—dead?"

"Very definitely dead," nodded Mr. Maltby, "only you will not see the body."

Smith's inclination to continue the ascent seemed to be cooling. He glanced upwards with apprehension, and then suddenly exclaimed:

"'Ere, is this a joke?"

"It did not present itself to me in that light," replied Mr. Maltby. "Nor, if you enter the room, is it likely to make *you* roar with laughter, Mr. Smith. You and I reached this house together, I recall, but you went away again for a period, so I have a longer acquaintance with it than you. It is not the pleasantest house I have ever been in. Well, why do you wait? Don't let me stop you."

Mr. Hopkins seized the tempting moment.

"Yes, is he coming down, or are you going up?" he asked with a glassy grin.

"Shurrup!" grunted the cockney. There was a short pause, then he inquired, "Which bloody room is it?"

"Bloody," repeated Mr. Maltby reflectively. "A most appropriate term. But I shall not tell you which sanguinary room this is, Mr. Smith. No, I shall let you find that out for yourself."

He resumed his interrupted journey down to the hall, but before the cockney resumed his own journey he shot out one more question.

"Attic?"

"Why should you think that?" queried Mr. Maltby.

"Why not?"

"And, also, why?"

"Bah!" grunted Smith, and went up.

No one spoke for several seconds after he had gone. In a mood to ask questions, David forebore. But Mr. Hopkins, when he had fortified himself with a cigarette, showed less restraint.

"I say—was—was that true?" he inquired in a low tone. "About that room?"

"Ask that gentleman over there," answered Mr. Maltby with a cynical glance towards the painting over the mantelpiece. "He might tell you."

"Of course, if you want my opinion," muttered Mr. Hopkins, "everybody's dotty."

"Before many hours, everybody may be dottier," said Mr. Maltby dryly, and turned to David. "I looked in on our patient on my way down."

"Thomson?"

"I didn't like his appearance."

"I'm sorry to hear you say that. Do you think he's really bad?"

"Well, if I had to guess his temperature, I should put it between 102 and 103."

"Whew!"

"And still rising."

"I've seen a man go up to 107," observed Mr. Hopkins.

"Ah, but that was probably in India," suggested David gently.

"As a matter of fact, young man, it was in India, though I don't care very much for your tone. Bombay. Stayed up for three days. But he got through it."

"Then we may hope Mr. Thomson will get through it. Hallo, here comes our rather rude friend back again, and with my sister behind him."

Smith looked surly and worried as he descended the stairs, but Lydia was all smiles. She appeared to be driving the cockney before her, and half-way down the staircase she called out:

"Silence, all of you, for a speech!"

David and she had not parted the best of friends, but now he welcomed her reappearance, for she struck a pleasant and much needed contrast to the prevailing atmosphere of nerviness and gloom.

"Hear, hear!" he murmured.

"Don't be a goat, you can't say 'Hear, hear' before a speech begins!" she exclaimed.

"It's the safest time to say it with *your* speeches," he replied with a grin. "There's no earthly chance of saying it afterwards!"

"Don't pay any attention to the lad, it's only a brother speaking," responded Lydia. "Anyhow, whether I get any 'hear, hear's' or not, this is what I've got to say. We've reached a point, all of us, where we've got to come to a decision. What I mean is, we're all wandering around and about like a lot of lost sheep!"

"Eh?" blinked Mr. Hopkins.

"Yes, I thought *you'd* take that up," said Lydia. "You've done a spot of wandering, haven't you?" She rejoiced secretly in his guilty flush. "And so has Mr. Smith here. I found *him* wandering, too. This was our brilliant conversation in the passage above. 'Hallo,' I said. 'Hallo,' he said. 'Where are you going?' I said. 'I don't know,' he said. 'Then why go?' I said. That stumped you, Mr. Smith, didn't it? So down we came, and *that* little bit of the world's history was over."

"Ah, then it was you, Miss Carrington, who returned this particular sheep to the fold?" smiled Mr. Maltby, while David thought, "What's happened to sis? She's gone all witty!"

"Corse, *you* all know wotcher torkin' abart," mumbled the cockney.

"I don't quite, though it sounds good," admitted David. "What's this decision we're supposed to make, Lydia?"

"Why, to *stop* wandering about like the lost sheep," she explained, "and to organise ourselves into a normally functioning community before this extraordinary situation entirely demoralises us."

She paused for approval or dissent. From Mr. Maltby she received approval.

"Miss Carrington's idea seems to me most sensible," he nodded. "Provided, of course, it can be carried out."

"Then you go on with it," replied Lydia, "and show us how it can be carried out."

But this time Mr. Maltby shook his head.

"That's not such a good idea," he answered. "For the moment I think I will content myself with a watching brief."

"He's right," added David. "It's your baby, Lydia."

"Very well. Here's luck to the baby!" she said. "If it dies in infancy it won't be my fault. Firstly, then, I decide that we pass a vote of confidence in our behaviour."

"You might remember that if my sister isn't intelligent, she's pretty," murmured David.

"And you are neither!" Lydia shot back. "And what I'm saying now *is* intelligent! Half our trouble is that we've got guilty consciences——"

"'Oo 'as?" interrupted Smith.

"You can be excluded if you like, Mr. Smith," retorted Lydia. "Perhaps your conscience is less sensitive. But *I* have. I keep on thinking, 'How simply awful of us to be here like this, using the house as if it was ours,' and then trying to make excuses for myself——"

"Same here," interposed David.

"What about you, Mr. Hopkins?" asked Lydia. "You've taken possession of another of the bedrooms. Does it worry you at all, or not?"

Mr. Hopkins frowned rather suspiciously. He was not quite sure about anything.

"Well, I had to get dry, same as the rest, didn't I?" he demanded.

"Then it didn't worry you?"

"I don't say—well, one's got to admit the whole position is rather peculiar."

"Only it doesn't worry you?"

"As much as you, I dare say."

"Then it worries you. And you, Mr. Smith?"

"I'm out o' this," replied Smith.

"That leaves just you, Mr. Maltby. How is your conscience getting along?"

"If I am worried, it is not by my conscience," said Mr. Maltby. "Just the same, Miss Carrington, I realise your point and consider it a good one psychologically, for it is impossible to function fluently through a sense of guilt. That is why any general, however wrong he may be—take Napoleon, to avoid the politics of mere contemporary examples—must believe in himself to be successful, or dupe himself into such a belief. Indeed, that is the main job of all politicians who, through their own inefficiency, muddle nations into war. If they do not fool themselves into the assumption that they are God-fearing idealists, they will never get the millions who must pay for their damage to believe the same thing, and they will lose the war."

"Here endeth the first lesson," murmured David.

"Then you think I'm fooling myself?" inquired Lydia.

"No, I am sure you are not fooling yourself; the lesson was not intended for you," replied the old man. "Probably I just wanted to hear my own voice. So, returning from great wars to smaller conflicts, I see no logical reason why we should depress ourselves with a sense of guilt since it is quite impossible for any of us to leave here to-night."

"Thank you for those kind words," smiled Lydia gratefully. "You are being a tremendous help, and to-morrow I shall kiss you under the mistletoe! Now, then, that vote of confidence! Hands up for a good opinion of ourselves!"

Five hands went up. Smith's went up last, as though suddenly fearing to be left behind. Lydia laughed.

"Carried unanimously!"

"Can we say that?" asked David, and reminded her that there were two more hands upstairs.

"Oh, I'll go proxy for them," she answered, and held up both her hands. "Right one for Miss Noyes, whose approval I've got in advance, and left one for Mr. Thomson. Poor Mr. Thomson, I feel sure, would do anything I asked him to. So the next step—what's the next step? Please go on helping me, Mr. Maltby. I'm really not quite as efficient as I seem."

"Well," suggested Mr. Maltby, "perhaps the next step is to justify that good opinion?"

"How right! You shall have two kisses under the mistletoe. I might even make it three if you'd tell me how the justification proceeds!"

"A good start would be to keep a detailed account of the damage."

"Mr. Maltby, you're a genius! I don't know what we'd have done without you. Yes, we must appoint an Hon. Treasurer. Who'll be Hon. Treasurer? I rather think that ought to be your job, David."

"Before I accept the Hon.," said David cautiously, "what exactly does the Hon. Individual do?"

"He jots down all we take and all we break, with the cost thereof. Tea for so many, so much. Dinner for so many, so much. Broken cups, so many, so much. There'll be plenty of those! And then, before we go——"

"If we ever go," murmured David.

"——we tot up the total, add so much for use of bedrooms, bathroom, towels, serviettes, table-cloths——"

"We're not taking the towels, serviettes and tablecloths away with us——"

"No, but they'll have to be washed."

"How about the wear and tear of the carpets, not to mention furniture and other messuages?"

"Don't be tedious, darling. Where was I? We tot up the total, add something for whatever I said, plus a good Christmas tip, and leave the amount on—where?—I know, the mantelpiece under that watchful old gentleman with the splendid head of hair who is spying on us to see how we behave ourselves. Well, David, do you take the post?"

"O.K. I take it."

"Good. You won't forget, when you're doing the accounts, that your job is an Hon. one? You are working for glory, not for profit! Now, then, next. What's next? Domestic staff. Who can cook? I can a bit, but I loathe it."

Mr. Hopkins cleared his throat. He felt it was necessary for his dwindling reputation to make some contribution.

"Well, I've cooked round a camp fire," he said. "You know. Roughing it. But—well—I'm not quite sure——"

"Then perhaps I'll have to cook, after all," sighed Lydia. "Which means that you'll get things out of tins warmed up."

"I think I ought to do something," replied Mr. Hopkins.

"You can and you shall. You and Mr. Smith can lay tables and so on."

"Yes, that's right, I'll be the butler!" exclaimed Mr. Hopkins, with sudden enthusiasm. "That's the idea. Carry trays up to the invalids——"

"You can carry Mr. Thomson's tray up," said Lydia curtly. "And that, Mr. Maltby, leaves *you* free to play the part of Father Christmas!"

"I am afraid I should make a very poor Father Christmas, Miss Carrington," answered the old man. "We shall have to rule out Santa Claus this year."

"I have no intention of ruling out Santa Claus," retorted Lydia. "Though, of course, we won't insist that *you* play the rôle. I am going to hang up my stocking, and I shall be bitterly disappointed if I find nothing in it. Make a note of that, David. Yes, and let me warn you all, so you won't feel ashamed of yourselves on Christmas morning, that *I'm* giving presents!"

She made the statement with good-humoured defiance. Mr. Maltby, whose mind dwelt beneath surfaces, had noted the defiance all along—defiance of the situation which, in her own words, was attempting to demoralise them. "I wonder how that very excellent spirit will behave," he reflected, "when—or if—the situation develops?" Meanwhile, he awarded her high marks for her present attitude.

David, on the other hand, wondered whether the attitude were not exceeding its logical limit.

"I'm all for good cheer and all that, sis," he commented, "but don't let's overdo it."

"Why not?" she returned. "Isn't everything being overdone? I'm fighting the absurd exaggeration of the snow and of our position with its own weapons. I'm *going* to overdo it. I feel like Noel Coward's song, 'Something To Do With Spring,' where the grass was too green and the lambs looked like rural Deans. Only, of course, this is Something To Do With Christmas. To-morrow is going to be a riot, folks, and that's another thing we'll have to talk about. The Christmas programme. We're not going to sit on our thumbs all day, if this snow keeps on. We'll have a party and a dance. But first things first. Is anybody getting hungry? Come along, staff. Step on it. We mustn't keep the family waiting for dinner. I may not be honest and sober, but I *am* punctual!"

Mr. Hopkins and Mr. Smith glanced at each other, then followed the girl obediently into the kitchen.

CHAPTER XI

JESSIE CONTINUES HER DIARY

"LYDIA really is a nice person, one of the nicest I have ever known. I think she knows I'm rather lonely up here, though she doesn't know I'm also frightened, well, sometimes I'm frightened, not all the time, so she keeps on popping in to say hallo and give me bits of news, how she does it with all the other things she's got to do I don't know. She's taken on the cooking and the general managing now, that's why she's so busy.

"She came up and told me about it during what she called 'her first moment off.' 'They all took it splendidly,' she said, 'and I believe we're going to have a happy Christmas, after all.'

"I asked her what she'd said to them, and she rattled it all off in two minutes. Her brother backed her up, as she thought he would, and Mr. Maltby was also a sport. I wonder whether Lydia feels the same way that I do about him, I must ask her next time. He's a nice old man really, I think, if only he wouldn't look right through you. I'm sure he sees right through me and out the other side, he gives me a funny sensation. What's more, I believe he knows it, because I caught him looking at me once, not through me that time, as though he was thinking about me in a way I don't like. I don't mean like Mr. Hopkins thinks about me, *of course not*, but in a way that made me remember I was once told I was psychic. I hope I'm not. Anyhow, I don't know how to spell it.

"But I was writing about Lydia. She said David and Mr. Maltby backed her up at once, but the other two only did so (she thought) because they were sort of roped in. They are helping her in the kitchen, laying the table, etc., but she says they're like brewing storms. David is making out lists and things, because of course we're paying for what we're taking, I told her I could pay my share, and I think he's also working out some games for to-morrow. It all seems very funny, though after all why shouldn't we enjoy ourselves if we can? If we're still here on Christmas night there'll be a dance. I wish my foot were better, I think it might be by then. I *can* dance, anyway!

"She didn't know what Mr. Maltby was doing when I asked her, but she thought he'd gone to see how poor Mr. Thomson was getting on. When I begin to feel sorry for myself I think of Mr. Thomson, he's worse. I was glad she thought he'd gone to see Mr. Thomson because I thought I'd heard some one moving in the passage, and if it hadn't been Mr. Maltby, well, who would it have been? I had one idea, but I'm not going to write what it was!

"I hope she'll be in again soon, though even then she won't be able to stop. She popped back once after she left to ask if I liked brown bread or white.

"One thing I'm glad of. I haven't had that horrible suffocating feeling again, though once I nearly got it. It seems so silly. This is such a lovely room, really. It's the kind of bedroom you'd choose for Christmas time, in fact, all this ought to be ideal. Oak beams, log fires, old-fashioned beds, and snow—it's what you want every year and never get except on Christmas cards. I expect, as Lydia said, it's the company that's wrong, that is, some of it. If we could have chosen who we wanted it would have been different.

"Yes, but then I mightn't have been chosen myself!

"Some one's coming. It's Lydia. I know her step."

"She brought a large cup of bovril, and it certainly has taken away that sinking feeling! I was hungrier than I knew, and from what she said they all seem to feel the same way about things downstairs. 'You never saw such greedy eyes,' she said, 'as when I took the first course into the dining-room!' 'Didn't one of the men take it in?' I said, because she'd told me they were going to do that kind of work. 'No, they were more trouble than they were worth,' said she, 'so I put them in their places and told them to stick there! They did nothing but get in the way and bicker.' 'What about Mr. Thomson, what are you giving him?' I asked. 'He's drowsy, he didn't want anything,' she answered, and I said, 'Poor Mr. Thomson, but just as well, feed a cold and starve a fever.' I don't know why I'm writing all this conversation down, but it gives me something to do and stops me thinking too much, that's one of my troubles, I think too much.

"I hope poor Mr. Thomson isn't going to get really bad, that *would* land us in a mess, because we can't get a doctor. I wonder why this house hasn't got a telephone? It's funny, but when people are in trouble you like them more, I didn't like him (Mr. Thomson) in the train, but I like him better now just because I'm sorry for him. He wants a sweetheart if ever a person did, but I'm sure even if he died I wouldn't like him enough for that. I've just read what I've just written, but anyhow I know what I mean.

"I asked Lydia what the next course was going to be, but she wouldn't tell me, it's got to be a surprise. The fire's gone down a bit, I'll ask her to make it up when she comes back. No, why should I ask her to? She does everything. My foot feels better, I'm sure I can do it....

"Well, I did do it, but it wasn't as easy as I thought. Anyhow, the fire's blazing away now, and——"

"It *was* a surprise! I don't mean the salmon (tinned), but David who brought it. 'I thought I'd save my sister the trouble this time,' he said. 'I hope you don't mind, she's working like a horse.'

" 'Of course I don't mind. Yes, she is,' I said. 'She'll be dead by the time she goes to bed to-night.'

" 'Not if I know her,' he said, 'she's as strong as an ox.' Then he laughed and said, 'I'm sorry if I'm mixing my animals.'

" 'I wish I could help her,' I said.

" 'Well, that's more your bad luck than hers,' he answered, 'how are you feeling?'

" 'I'm all right,' I said.

"Then he laughed again, and said, 'Yes, you always say that, don't you?'

" 'Well, I am,' I said. 'I got out of bed just now and made up the fire, only don't tell your sister, will you, or she'd never forgive me!'

" 'I'm not sure that I'll forgive you, either,' he said. 'You've got to look after yourself.' He could have gone then quite easily, there was nothing for him to stay for, but he seemed rather to like to stay, and somehow it was very nice. He looked round the room, and said, 'And I'm not sure that I'm so sorry for you, either, it's nice and comfortable here, and cheerful. We're not quite so cheerful downstairs.'

" 'Aren't you?' I asked.

" 'Not by a long chalk,' he answered. 'Half the time we sit in gloomy silence, and then some one makes a funny remark—it's generally me—and nobody laughs.'

" 'I ought to be there,' I told him. 'I'd laugh!'

" 'I believe you would,' he replied. 'Even Mr. Hopkins isn't telling his usual yarns about when he was in India, my boy, what, what!'

" 'Was that one of your funny remarks?' I said. 'Anyhow, you see, I'm laughing. But I should have thought Mr. Hopkins would have talked enough for everybody, he did in the train.'

" 'Yes, he's in his element in trains,' said David, I call him David here, but not actually yet, 'but this house seems to have dried him up.'

" 'Well, I think he's best dried up,' I said. 'I never want to hear his beastly voice again!'

"I expect I said it with more meaning than I meant to, because he suddenly looked at me rather hard.

" 'Hallo, why did you say that?' he asked.

"I certainly didn't want to tell him why. It had just come suddenly. I know a lot about men, too much I expect, but Mr. Hopkins is the sort I really *can't* stand, I don't know how to deal with them, maybe they're all right really and can't help it, I've got views about people not being able to help themselves, but even so it doesn't make any difference to how you feel about them, you can't help your feelings either. Isn't it awful the way my pen, pencil rather, runs away with me? Now I've got to look back to see where I was!...

" 'Nothing,' I said.

"But he went on looking at me rather hard. It's funny what thoughts come. I was thinking, 'I do hope my nose isn't shiny!'

" 'Miss Noyes,' he said, 'people don't say things like that for nothing!'

" 'Sometimes they do,' I answered, 'if they're like me.'

" 'Look here,' he replied, 'I want you to tell me something. Will you?'

" 'I can't say till I know what it is.'

" 'Has he been worrying you?'

"That was pretty quick of him, unless I'd really given the show away even more than I'd thought, and it got me all confused so that I said something silly like this, 'No, yes, no, of course not.'

"'You're not very good at fibs,' he said.

"'I don't know what you mean,' I answered, 'and I think you'd better go down again now, don't think I'm turning you out, only isn't it time you tried them again with something funny, perhaps they'll laugh this time.'

"'And you're not very good at pretending you don't know what people mean when all the time you jolly well do,' he said. He wouldn't be put off. 'No, it's *not* time to go down and be funny just yet, and you do know what I mean!'

"'All right, suppose I do, but now you tell *me* something,' I said. 'What makes you think Mr. Hopkins would worry me?'

"'Shall I tell you bluntly,' he asked, 'or shall I wrap it up in cotton-wool?'

"'You can tell me bluntly,' I said, 'no, wrap it up in cotton-wool.'

"'No, I'm not going to,' he said. 'I should think Mr. Hopkins would worry anybody, but particularly a—a charming girl like you.'

"That's what he said. It was silly that I turned red, but I couldn't help it. Of course, I had to answer something, so I told him, like an idiot, that Mr. Hopkins hadn't worried me, but I was afraid that he might, and somehow that made it worse than ever and I got as red as a beetroot.

"'The damned bounder,' he said.

"He said it so fiercely that he almost frightened me.

"'You're not going to make a row,' I begged him.

"'I'd like to punch his nose,' he answered.

" 'You can like to, certainly, but you won't, will you?' I asked. 'Promise me!'

"He promised me, and then I told him that I thought he really ought to go this time. Not that I wanted him to, I'm sure he understood that, but because of the others. And so, after a few more words, he went.

"One reason I thought he ought to go was because people are so rotten at thinking things. Of course, they're generally right."

CHAPTER XII

DINNER CON FUOCO

WHEN David returned to the dining-room he found Lydia fighting courageously, but not very successfully, against the gloom. Mr. Maltby, who occasionally lent her his aid, seemed to have gone right back into his shell, and was busy with his thoughts; her conversation, therefore, was at the mercy of Mr. Hopkins and Smith, who were a blight on any company. Alone, each would have been trying enough. Together, they formed a source of constant, nervy irritation not only to others but to themselves. Mr. Hopkins was the worst. His attempts to conceal the obvious fact that he was ill at ease had turned him spiteful, and, forgetful of the danger of inciting the cockney, or else unable to control himself, he was visiting his spitefulness on that inflammatory individual. He had some cause.

"Now, then, *must* you dig your elbows into my face?" he rasped angrily.

It had been a mistake of Lydia's to place Smith in the chair next to him. Her idea had been that by this arrangement they would lose the incitement of seeing each other across the table, but it was a good effort that had gone wrong.

"Keep yer fice up and yer won't git 'em," answered Smith.

"I have to eat, my man!"

"Not so much of 'my man'! So do I 'ave to eat, but I don't keep bobbin' me fice up and dahn!"

"Impudence! Maybe not, but you keep wagging your elbows in and out!"

"'Oose elbows are they?"

"Come to that, sir, whose face is it? The face is mine, and the elbows are yours, and I am simply asking you to keep your elbows because I don't want them!"

"Well, I don't want your fice."

Lydia interposed.

"Perhaps," she suggested patiently, "your limbs and your faces would get less mixed up if you moved your two chairs a little farther apart?"

"I ain't goin' to move mine," mumbled the cockney. " 'E can move 'is."

Mr. Hopkins was beyond the wisdom of concession.

"Why should I move mine any more than you should move yours?" he demanded. "Really, in all my life, I never heard such rudeness!"

"It is a rude world," murmured Mr. Maltby.

"Thank you for nothing!" snapped Mr. Hopkins.

David had lingered in the doorway. Now, as he resumed his seat, Lydia turned to him with relief.

"Welcome back to the loving family," she exclaimed. "I haven't *quite* given up my idea of a happy Christmas, David, but Peace and Goodwill have got to get a move on! How are things on the upper deck?"

"Brighter than on the lower," smiled her brother. "You appear to have missed me. Shall I revert to desperate remedies and try to be funny?"

"The situation isn't quite as desperate as that. You were a long time upstairs."

"Yes. I took pity on loneliness."

"And how is Her Loneliness?"

"I think she's better. She got out of bed and made up the fire—oh, but I wasn't to mention that!"

"Why didn't you save her the trouble, and make up the fire yourself?"

"Because, sister mine, I wasn't present at the stoking operation. It was all done before the salmon arrived. By the way, how much is salmon per tin? We are demolishing two tins, I understand."

"One and sixpence, about."

"Then two tins will be three bob, about, to add to the charge sheet."

"And two more tins of pineapple chunks will be another bob to add to the charge sheet. Our bill's mounting as rapidly as the snow!"

"And the one won't stop till the other does," said David. "It's a good thing I drew out three thousand pounds just before I left."

Lydia turned to Smith, who had raised his head.

"Another example of my brother's humour," she assured him. "He hasn't even three thousand pennies."

The conversation continued spasmodically. Brother and sister were doing their best. When the salmon went and the pineapple came, Mr. Hopkins suddenly rose, shoving his chair back noisily and exclaiming, "Look here, look here, I'm not doing anything, I'll take that up." Lydia and David exchanged significant glances.

"I don't think Mr. Thomson will want any," said Lydia, deliberately obtuse.

"Thomson? Eh?" jerked Mr. Hopkins. "Oh! Well, what about Miss Noyes?"

"I'm going to take hers up," answered Lydia.

And then, all at once, Mr. Hopkins burst, and the storm for which Mr. Maltby had been waiting arrived. He was surprised that it had been delayed so long.

"What the hell's the matter with me?" Mr. Hopkins cried, his face growing purple. "What's everybody got against me? Told to do this, told to do that, mustn't do this, mustn't do that! Mustn't I even volunteer to lend a hand with a tray? Am I—am I a leper?"

"Please don't get so excited, Mr. Hopkins," begged Lydia apprehensively.

"Who's excited?"

"I only thought I'd like to see how Miss Noyes is getting along."

"You didn't want to see how she was getting along when your brother offered to take the tray up!" retorted the angry man. If he regretted his outburst, he seemed unable now to draw back. The tide was sweeping over him. "I expect *he* wanted to see how she was getting along, too, eh? Yes, and he was a damn long time about it!"

"I don't think I care for that remark, Mr. Hopkins," said David.

"I don't care whether you care or not, I'm sick of being told what I'm to do and what I'm not to do! We're all equal here, aren't we? Who's given anybody the reins? Am I the horse?"

"No, the blinkin' donkey," said Smith.

Mr. Hopkins swung round fiercely.

"Now, then, I don't want any more of *your* impudence!" he cried. "You're the one that ought to be sat upon! Yes, and why aren't you? Coming here and lying, and everybody sitting down under it——"

"'Ere, wot's that?" interrupted the cockney, his ugly face darkening.

"Oh, shut up!"

"'Oo's lyin'?"

"You, and you know it! *Now* shut up!"

Smith's fingers began to press into the tablecloth as though he were trying to hold them down.

"I'm to shut up, am I?" he glared. "I'll shut up when you've tiken that back."

"I'm not going to take anything back," said Mr. Hopkins.

"Oh, yer won't?"

"No."

Mr. Maltby cleared his throat. "I think, gentlemen——" he began. But he got no further. Smith cut him short.

"'Ere, you keep aht of it!" he cried. "This is me and 'im! I don't let bags o' flabby flesh call me a liar, and I ain't lettin' it go this time!" He turned back to Mr. Hopkins. "When did I lie? Go on, let's 'ave it."

"There's no need for me to remind you," answered Mr. Hopkins, struggling to keep his voice steady.

"Ain't there? Well, that's where I see dif'rent, see? When did I lie?"

"All right, damn you, if you want it you'll get it. When you said you weren't on our train."

"Oh, *you* was on the trine?"

"*I've* not denied it?"

"Well, why should I?"

"You want that, too?"

"Go on!" Mr. Hopkins hesitated. His face was now more purple than ever, but not only with anger. He was struggling against fear. "See, yer ain't got nothink ter say! Yer a gas-bag, that's wot yer are, and fer tuppence I'd tike yer bloody nose and twist if orf——"

"Because you're a murderer, that's why!" screamed Mr. Hopkins. "Because it was you who killed that man—now you *have* got it——"

The next moment he fell back as Smith's fist caught his chin. "Quick, David," said Lydia quietly, while Mr. Maltby rose from his chair. But David was already on his feet, and was hurrying round to the other side of the table.

Mr. Hopkins made an effort, but before he could recover Smith was on him again. Lydia never forgot Smith's face at that instant. She described it afterwards as "just sheerly homicidal." As Mr. Hopkins's arms wound despairingly round him the cockney's fingers pressed on his throat. Mr. Hopkins's face did not make a pleasant memory, either.

"I shouldn't worry, Mr. Smith," came Mr. Maltby's voice, with a calmness that was almost unbelievable because of its inappropriateness. "It's Mr. Hopkins who is the murderer." Smith's fingers paused in their pressure. "Let him go, we'll manage the rest."

Behind Smith's back Mr. Maltby made a swift sign to David, and David, wise to the ruse, threw himself upon the cockney, while Mr. Hopkins slipped limply to the floor. But the cockney had a brute's strength, and the instinct of self-preservation coupled with a ferocious anger at having been duped made him fight like a tiger. Chairs went over. So did Mr Maltby when he met one of the chairs on his way into the fray. Lydia seized somebody's leg, to find it was her brother's. Momentarily released by this mishap, Smith leapt away, snatched a knife from the table, and escaped from the room.

In a flash Lydia was after him. When she reached the hall she found it empty. She did not look for the frenzied fugitive, but raced up the stairs without stopping till she was outside Jessie's door. Then she paused, took a deep, much needed breath, and called through:

"All right in there?"

"Yes! Is anything happening?" came the response from the bed.

"No, I just came to inquire. Bring you your next course in a minute or two."

She stood hesitating. She did not believe that Smith had ascended the stairs, but she felt she could not leave the door till she was certain.

From below came sounds. David and Mr. Maltby had now recovered, and were beginning their search. "Lydia! Where are you?" It was David's anxious voice. She realised that she must show herself, to allay that anxiety, and slipped to the top of the stairs. "Up here," she called down softly. "I don't think he came this way."

Then she heard an exclamation.

"No, he didn't!" David called back. "Stay where you are."

The exclamation had come from Mr. Maltby. An icy draught had led him into the kitchen towards the back door, and a window by the back door was open. Somehow or other, Smith had scrambled out. That, at any rate, was the inference. The back door itself was blocked by a snowdrift.

David joined the old man. For a moment they stared out into the darkness flecked with whirling white. Mr. Maltby raised his hand to close the window.

"Good riddance!" muttered David.

"It's a pity he's got that knife," answered Mr. Maltby.

"The knife won't do him much good out there," replied David. "I wonder how long he'll last!"

He also wondered why Mr. Maltby did not close the window.

"No. For a moment I thought … well, this open-air treatment won't help our health."

He began to pull the window down. Then he paused again. A terrified shriek pierced the darkness, lending it a new horror.

"My God, what was that!" gasped David.

He strained forward, but Mr. Maltby shoved him away and closed the window resolutely.

"We'll get back to the dining-room," he said. "We've things to talk about."

CHAPTER XIII

EXHIBIT B

THEY found Mr. Hopkins sitting on the dining-room floor looking very sorry for himself. He was no longer purple; he was white; and his eyes were watering. He also seemed to be experiencing some difficulty in swallowing.

"That fellow nearly choked me," he spluttered.

"You were fortunate that he did not quite choke you," replied Mr. Maltby, without sympathy.

"I see, I'm in the wrong again!"

"Very much in the wrong again. I have never seen a more pitiable example of lack of control and lack of intelligence. We all knew that Smith had murdered a man—probably by the same method by which he nearly murdered you—but Smith did not know we knew until you told him——"

"He knew *I* knew," mumbled Mr. Hopkins.

"I doubt, from his attitude, whether he knew himself," retorted Mr. Maltby.

While Mr. Hopkins looked incredulous, David looked almost equally astonished.

"Surely, sir!" he exclaimed. "If he didn't know, why did he leave the train in such a hurry?"

"Yes, and lie about it," added Mr. Hopkins, gulping. "Tell me that!"

"One reason you do not know yet," answered Mr. Maltby, "but the other should be obvious. He knew he had hurt his man. He did not know, I am reasonably convinced, the full extent of the damage. Even assault, however, is a criminal offence, so naturally he left the train in a hurry, and naturally he denied ever having been on the train. Do you conceive that if he had had a definite murder on his conscience, and had assumed our own equal knowledge of it, he would have acted as he did? He was anxious and worried. You, Mr. Hopkins, gave him particular cause for anxiety. But he thought that, for the time being, he was better off with us than—where he now is, out in the snow."

"I dare say you're right," said David, after a pause. "But I still can't quite follow his attitude. I mean, of course, until this final flare up. I think, in his position, I would have risked the snow."

"But you do not know his position," smiled Mr. Maltby.

"You mean—that other reason you mentioned for his leaving the train?"

Mr. Maltby nodded.

"That has played a very important part in Mr. Smith's movements here. Yes, in the end he would probably have risked the snow in any case, and I dare say he had already decided on his method of escape—through the window. Only, you see, I had not intended to give him the chance. But for you, Mr. Hopkins, we should have had our murderer locked up to-night, instead of wandering around outside loose with a knife."

"What was the other reason?" asked David.

"I will come to that in a minute. Where is your sister?"

"Upstairs, I think."

"You had better go and see. No, wait. She was going to take some pineapple up to Miss Noyes. Take it up yourself now, Mr. Carrington, and suggest that your sister stays with Miss Noyes and keeps her company for a little while. But I want you down again as soon as you can come, please."

"Right," said David. "That's a good idea."

"Your sister has plenty of pluck—I admire her," said Mr. Maltby, while David took the long delayed plate of pineapple, "but perhaps there is no need to increase the strain she already has on her mind. I wonder, by the way, whether she heard—what we heard? If you can find out tactfully, will you do so?"

"That's a good idea, too," answered David as he left the room.

Mr. Hopkins, who had now risen from the carpet and was in the act of taking a sip of water, showed signs of returning agitation.

"Heard—what you heard?" he queried. "What was that?"

"You heard nothing yourself, then?"

"When?"

"While we were out of the room? Half a minute before we returned."

"I don't know. My head was buzzing. It still is. I—I did think——"

"Yes?"

"The wind's rising, isn't it?"

"It wasn't the wind."

"Then what was it? I'm asking you! Why do you keep on going round and round the bush with me?"

"Because, Mr. Hopkins, whenever anything has to be faced, you always go round and round the bush yourself, and so I have to go round and round the bush to catch you up. You did hear something?"

"Yes, yes. Well, that is, I thought I did. But I put it down to the wind, or my head, or both. Does that satisfy you?"

"What did it sound like, apart from the wind or your head?"

"A—a shriek."

"It was a shriek."

"Eh?"

"A very unearthly shriek."

"Unearthly? You don't mean——?"

"I thought you did not believe in ghosts and spooks and suchlike bosh? I thought you had exploded them? In Rangoon, if I remember rightly?"

"Who said anything about ghosts?" retorted Mr. Hopkins, trying to fight back.

"Listen," said Mr. Maltby. "You have been through an unpleasant experience, and for that I make allowances. But do you recall that, while in the train, you told at least half a dozen stories in which you figured as something of a hero? You endured worse snow than this without a murmur in Dawson City. You shot a tiger while it was springing at you in your pet corner of the world, India. You told a bandit in China where to get off. I quote your own expression—it is not one of mine. You taught a Zulu warrior chess. Cannot you recapture a little of that spirit here and now? I assure you, Mr. Hopkins, you will need it during the next few minutes while I am telling you certain things—including, I may mention, my interpretation of that shriek.... Ah, Mr. Carrington. You have been quick. How is your sister? All right?"

David nodded as he entered the room.

"Everything O.K.," he answered. "She's staying with Miss Noyes. She heard what we heard, and agreed it was best."

"That was sensible of her."

"She did make one provision, though."

"What was it?"

"That she wasn't to be kept perpetually in the dark."

"We are all somewhat in the dark," replied Mr. Maltby. "I propose now, however, to try and find a little light. Wait a moment."

He left the room, and for a minute David and Mr. Hopkins had to endure each other alone.

"Coming round?" asked David.

"I am obliged for the kind inquiry," responded Mr. Hopkins. "I am coming round."

"That fellow was pretty dangerous."

"Again, I am obliged for the information."

"Sorry I spoke!"

They fell into a profitless silence till Mr. Maltby came back. He was carrying three objects which he placed carefully on the table, clearing a small space for their reception. One was a hammer. The second was a black leather letter-case. The third was a torn envelope from which protruded a torn sheet of paper. His companions regarded them with interest.

"Exhibit A," began the old man, touching the hammer. "I found it on my way here, near this house. It was partially, but not completely, covered by the snow. Does that suggest anything to either of you?"

"It suggests something to me," answered David.

"What?"

"That it must have been left there or dropped quite recently, otherwise it would have been completely covered by the snow."

"A good mark for that, Mr. Carrington. Your conclusion is the same as mine. I picked it up and I put it in my pocket. We will return to it when I describe a little incident. Exhibit B." He pointed to the black letter-case. "I found *that* in the attic. We will return to the letter-case, also, when I describe another little incident. Exhibit C." He touched the torn envelope and paper. "I found that in the waste-paper basket in the room occupied by Mr. Thomson. The same comment applies.

"I have mentioned these three articles in the order in which I found them, but we will deal first with the second exhibit—B— because that applies to the subject of our first inquiry. Namely,

Smith. I think I can reconstruct his complete story—that is, from just before he left the train to just after he left here finally. At least, we hope finally, but there may be more of his story to come. The other two exhibits, A and C, belong to a second story, a good deal of which I think we can also reconstruct. There will be blanks in the second story, however, which we will try to fill in later. It is the story of this house, and of how it came to be left in the condition in which we found it."

"You think you've discovered that?" exclaimed David.

"I think I have partially discovered it. And, curiously, it is the conclusion of Smith's story that has supplied, or confirmed, a vital detail in the second. Yes, unless I am very much mistaken, at that conclusion the two stories touched. Our own personal stories, of course, are so far merely incidental."

"One moment, sir," interposed David.

"Well?"

"The conclusion of Smith's story. Do you mean—that scream?"

"If I am right, that is the point where the stories met. Now then. The first story. It began when a fellow called Smith, but who has probably been known to the police by many other names, killed W. T. Barling."

"Barling?" cried Mr. Hopkins. "How the devil do you know the name?"

"The name, but not any address, is on a card in the letter-case. No, don't touch it!" he added sharply, as Mr. Hopkins's hand stretched forward. "Don't touch anything! You can be sure that, ever since I have realised their significance, I have handled these exhibits most carefully. As I handled the bread-knife when I put it away. There may be useful fingerprints on some of these articles."

David noticed that the old man's eyes travelled for an instant to the hammer.

"The case also contains forty-four one-pound treasury notes," continued Mr. Maltby. "Worth a risk to a man of Smith's mentality. Still, we may be reasonably sure Smith did not realise the risk he was taking when he stole the case. Let me reconstruct Smith's actions, and you can tell me where my logic is faulty.

"Barling, in the compartment next to us, dozes in his corner. Smith is the only other person in the compartment, and realises his opportunity. Barling may have displayed his case before he slept, or Smith may merely have made a good guess. These crooks are clever at guessing, and quickly classify us from their particular angle. How was Barling dressed, Mr. Hopkins? Do you remember?"

"Eh? No! Yes, I do," jerked Mr. Hopkins. "Tweeds. Rather loud. That's right."

"Did he look like a sporting man?"

"Well, now you come to mention it—of course, I couldn't be sure——"

"I am not asking you to be sure. Just your impression."

"Well, that was my impression. That is to say, not at the time, but—well, now you come to mention it."

"Then it would fit our facts if Barling, a sporting man, had made a packet and had unwisely boasted about it. Anyway, Smith stole the case, but wasn't quite clever enough, and woke Barling up. There was a tussle——"

"We didn't hear anything," interrupted David.

"Did you hear anything while Smith's fingers were pressing Mr. Hopkins's throat?"

Mr. Hopkins looked startled, then gulped at the memory.

"It was a swift, quiet struggle. Probably the whole thing flared up in an instant, and before the two men realised it they were at each other's throats. Once Smith smells definite danger, he doesn't wait. He acts."

"My God, yes!" muttered Mr. Hopkins.

"Mr. Hopkins will corroborate me when I suggest that Smith's hands are strong enough to choke a man——"

"Yes, but if you don't mind——"

"I noticed his strong hands at once, just as I noticed his low forehead and the bluntness of the back of his head and neck. So, I repeat, it was a swift, quiet tussle. These two did not slam at each other and tumble about. Smith showed no visible bruises. There was no blood on his clothes. Also, as Mr. Carrington has just reminded us, we did not hear anything—no angry shout or cry of agony. Barling died through strangulation, and when Smith's hands had done their work and Barling had slid to the floor of the compartment—where you and the guard found him, Mr. Hopkins—Smith went through a moment of stupefaction. He did not know whether he had killed Barling. Perhaps he thought that unlikely. But he had done enough damage, and he did not wait to find out the full extent. He developed panic and fled from the train. And I followed him."

"I still don't know why you followed him," said David, as his mind went back to the moment.

"I am not sure that I could explain in a way you could understand," replied the old man. "We judge life by our own reactions and sensations, and the reactions and sensations of others are often mere incomprehensible theories." He paused, and again eyed the hammer. "Would you think, for instance, that there are certain people—one, I believe, actually in this house—who could get a violent sensation merely by receiving on their forehead the touch of an implement that had been used violently on somebody else?"

"Why, yes, I remember a case something like that!" exclaimed Mr. Hopkins unexpectedly. "It was in South America. An old woman was touched with a piece of broken wood and yelled out that she was falling. It was a bit of an aeroplane that had crashed."

For once Mr. Hopkins had related a story that was both appropriate and interesting.

"The same idea," nodded Mr. Maltby.

"But who's the person in this house who—you don't mean *me*?"

"No, not you. Or myself. I merely gave that psychic faculty as one example of the seemingly impossible. My own experience was not due to actual contact with any article. I left the train through a sequence of three connected sensations, one occurring so rapidly after the other that they created in me an ungovernable impulse. Naturally I had no idea at the time that a murder had been committed, otherwise I would have acted differently—but you will recall, Mr. Hopkins, that when you brought your news of the tragedy, I guessed the compartment it had occurred in, and was also able to indicate—then—its nature.

"The first sensation was an uneasiness I sometimes, but not always, receive when anything violent had just happened. I receive it sometimes when it is going to happen."

"Have you got it now?" inquired Mr. Hopkins.

"I am convinced that something is going to happen," replied Mr. Maltby, "but whether violent or not I cannot say. The second sensation was due, I now think, to a sound. So, after all, Barling may have made some sound caught faintly, but not decipherably, by my ear. The third was of a more obvious nature. It was due to my sudden sight of Smith himself. I knew without any evidence that here was a man running away, and that he needed catching. My mistake," he added whimsically, "was to imagine that I could catch him. As you know, I lost Smith. He melted away in the snow. And while I floundered after him, getting lost myself—and, as you will learn in due course, gaining my first glimpse of the second story—this is what Smith did.

"He reached the house. This house. He found the door open——"

"We didn't find it open," interrupted David. "It was closed, but not locked."

"Smith closed it."

"But how do you know it was open when Smith got here?" demanded Mr. Hopkins.

He was recovering a little of his self-assurance. His story of South America had been a mental tonic. Also, the tubes of his throat were nearly normal again.

Mr. Maltby smiled. "You are right. I do not know. I deduce it from my belief that Smith would not have entered the house otherwise. On the other hand, he might risk poking his head in through the open doorway. But I deduce it as well from another fact that comes in the second story. He got in. He found the place empty. He bolted up to the attic. He was in the attic when you arrived, Mr. Carrington. He was the person you heard inside the room, and who obviously would not reply to you when you called through the door."

"You mean he'd bunked up and locked himself in?"

"Probably he locked the door as he heard you coming. Then, finding that you were not leaving the house, and that he was trapped——"

"He had nothing to fear from me."

"Did he know that?"

"Of course not. That's a bad mark."

"He did not need a knowledge of his murder to fear every unknown person just then, particularly as he was trespassing in somebody else's house. He knew he had committed assault and theft. So when he found you were not leaving, he tried to escape. First he unlocked the attic door. No good. Voices below. Then, omitting to lock the attic door again—you remember you were able to enter the second time—he ran to the window and tried that. He got out somehow. I found the window open, just a crack. He had not closed it completely. There is a low roof on which he could have jumped, and the softness of the snow doubtless helped him. But I noticed, if you did not, that Smith was trying to conceal a slight limp."

"No, I didn't notice it," replied David, "but after my bad mark let me score a good one again. When he reached the ground, he met you?"

"Yes. A few seconds afterwards, I expect."

"But why did he return with you?"

"Yes, why didn't he complete his get-away?" added Mr. Hopkins. "Wasn't he a bit of a mug?"

"He had left the case behind," answered Mr. Maltby.

"Oh, so he had, of course—you found it. Where?"

"It was behind a trunk near the window. Probably he was examining it when you came along, Mr. Carrington. Maybe he did not know till then just how much was in it. But you gave him a shock, and as he made for the window and climbed on the trunk it slipped out of his hand or his pocket. Forty-four pounds. A tragic sum to lose after all that trouble. Worth coming back for with a harmless, unsuspicious old gentleman.... But the forty-four pounds are still here, on that table."

They looked at Exhibit B, bulging with the cost of a man's life.

"He went away again," recalled David.

"And returned again," replied Mr. Maltby. "That cry of 'Help' gave him a proper scare. I am not sure, however, whether his third visit was due to the case or the weather. It may have been a combination of both.

"But we do know how he tried to get up to the attic, and how first one of us and then another blocked the way—some consciously, some unconsciously. Miss Carrington, for instance, had no idea what this lost sheep was looking for when she turned it back! But Smith would have got up to his attic eventually, because he thought he had sized the situation up and was playing a patient, waiting game. You were the only person he had to watch, Mr. Hopkins. He did not know you had told us of the tragedy, any more than he knew the tragedy's full extent."

"Didn't he have to watch you, too?" asked David. "It was you who found his railway ticket."

"Ah, but, I was also playing a patient, waiting game," retorted Mr. Maltby. "You remember how I changed my attitude to him, in order to put him off his guard, and how I managed to get to the attic myself before he had any chance of doing so? I was curious about that attic after what you had told me, and when I came down I had found the letter-case.

"But I didn't want Smith to know I had found it until I had cogitated a little more about the ticklish situation. If Smith had gone to the attic just then, he would merely have found the door locked again. Later, after my little cogitation, I worked out another plan, and I unlocked the attic door. The plan was to follow Smith up when he made for his goal and to turn the key on him."

"He could have repeated his escape through the window."

"He might have done so. But there is a wooden shutter across the window now, and it is very completely screwed up. He would have had a job."

Then Mr. Maltby turned to Mr. Hopkins with a shrug.

"But all that is mere theory, for Smith has flown. And it was, perhaps, poetic justice that Smith's path to escape—if he does escape—should have taken the particular direction it did. Smith screamed, I am willing to wager, because he thought he had seen Mr. W. T. Barling's ghost."

CHAPTER XIV

EXHIBITS A AND C

MR. HOPKINS took his handkerchief from his pocket and mopped his brow. It was not the first time he had done so, but his brow had never needed the operation more acutely.

"W-what's that mean?" he asked.

"It means," answered Mr. Maltby, "that W. T. Barling is probably not the only person who has been murdered to-day, and that the body of the second murdered person is considerably nearer to us than Barling's as we sit here. It means that Smith, in his last flight, tripped over the body, and may now be a raving lunatic—with a knife—as well as a murderer."

"How do you know?"

"Because I nearly tripped over the body myself. But at the time I thought it was a log."

"Then, since you now believe it wasn't a log, shouldn't we go out and look for it?" inquired David quietly.

His calmness surprised him. He attributed it to the possibility that he was growing numb to horror. No numbness, however, was visible in the goggling eyes of Mr. Hopkins.

"If you look for it, you are not likely to have Smith's luck of finding it," replied Mr. Maltby. "In fact, you may find Smith instead, and become an addition to the growing casualty list."

"But——"

"As a good British citizen and stickler for the law you feel you have a duty to perform? In that case I won't detain you. Only remember, before you go on your wild goose chase, that the body is undoubtedly dead, while you have not received any proof yet that it exists at all."

"Well, can I have the proof?"

"No. There isn't any proof. Not, at least, in your sense of the word. But you can have the second story which I am waiting to tell, and the delay may reduce your chance of encountering Smith's knife. Shall I go on?"

"Please."

"Right. Story No. Two, Exhibit C."

He took the torn envelope from the table and carefully extracted the torn sheet, smoothing it out on his knee.

"I found this, as I have said, in the waste-paper basket of Thomson's bedroom. It is a portion of a torn up letter, and I will read you out the legible words:

> " 'DEAR CHARLES,
>   'I shall
> spend Christmas at
> stores for a week
> the items to you
> will be two of us
> daughter, and I enclo
> the cost. I expect
> Eve, probably
> just before dinner.
> ing about this vis … ' "

Replacing the fragment of letter in the fragment of envelope, Mr. Maltby continued:

"Unfortunately the signature is absent, so we do not know the name of the sender, but we may deduce the name of the recipient from this on the envelope: 'rles Shaw.' The letter, therefore, was from some unknown person to Charles Shaw, and the complete letter itself, up to the point where it breaks off, probably ran along these lines:

"'Dear Charles, I shall be coming to spend Christmas at'— wherever this is—'so get in stores for a week. I shall leave the items to you, but there will be two of us, myself and my daughter, and I enclose'—however much the writer actually enclosed—'to cover the cost. I expect to arrive on Christmas Eve, probably in the evening'—or afternoon—'just before dinner. Say nothing about this visit.'

"We may take it that Charles Shaw was the caretaker or servant here. We may also take it, I think, that he slept in the room now occupied by Thomson, as it was there I found the scrap of letter, and as that room has been recently occupied. A slightly moist toothbrush was in a glass, and the jug was full of water. I also noticed a pair of pyjamas hanging from a hook on the door.

"Very well, then. Charles receives this letter—it is a pity the date was torn off—and buys the necessary stores for a week, unconscious of the fact that some of the stores will eventually be used by a marooned party from a train. I am assuming, by the way, that Charles occupied this house alone in the absence of his master, and was alone when he received the letter, and was alone this morning when he got up. Does the bedroom you have commandeered, Mr. Hopkins, look as though anybody had slept in it lately?"

"I can't say that it does," replied Mr. Hopkins, after a moment's thought. "No, I can't say that it does. Several unpleasant cobwebs about."

"Then Charles is not as meticulous as he ought to be. How about the water jug and the water bottle?"

Mr. Hopkins thought again.

"Well, yes, of course!" he exclaimed suddenly. "I had a wash!"

"And found towels?"

"That's right. I didn't have to use my handkerchief!"

"Do you remember whether the towel you used was clean, or had it been used before? And was it a new cake of soap?"

"Towel clean, soap new."

"All of which suggests that the room has not been slept in lately, but was prepared for some one tonight. That fits the pattern. And your sister's room, Mr. Carrington? Can you help me there?"

"Yes," replied David. "She told me I was to add, 'To soiling two fresh towels, defacing one cake of soap, and use of nail-brush,' to the charge sheet."

Mr. Maltby nodded.

"Good. The background of the picture is coming. Having laid in the stores, the lonely Charles awaits the arrival of his master and his master's daughter. This morning he prepares two bed-rooms for them, but not as thoroughly as he might. He omits to remove sundry cobwebs. Does this suggest a flaw in Charles's character, or has he something on his mind? … Something on his mind? … I wonder whether Charles is ever worried by that picture in the hall?"

"What makes you say that?" asked David.

"I don't quite know," answered the old man. "I am groping my way through sensations as well as known or deduced facts. Probably Charles was used to loneliness, but it might give one a queer feeling to get up on Christmas Eve—all alone in a house like this—with snow all around, and still coming down—white without and black within—eh?—and, in the morning dusk, descending the stairs to that picture? Yes, it might. You remember, Mr. Carrington, how we have felt that that picture was watching us——"

"By God, I've felt that, too!" exclaimed Mr. Hopkins.

"Have you?"

"By God, I have!"

"This fellow's becoming more human and natural," reflected David. "I wonder whether, after all, fear's good for him?"

"Then Charles might have felt it," said Mr. Maltby.

"Yes, and the chap in the picture was *coming*," added Mr. Hopkins.

Mr. Maltby pursed his lips.

"Not necessarily," he replied. "We don't know that it is a picture of the owner of this house. It may be, but it may not be. There is something just pre-war about his suit. I should place his age at a little over sixty. Not such an enormous age, either, or so we like to think when we come to it. So if my sartorial knowledge is correct, that picture was painted over twenty years ago, and the subject of it would be about eighty-five to-day. Now that *is* an enormous age at which to be travelling about the wintry countryside at Christmas. Incidentally," he went on, with a sudden rather wicked little glance at David, "it ruins our romantic conception of the daughter. We want a few bright spots in our reconstruction." He turned for a moment to Exhibit C. "And this writing, though not very good, is not the writing of an octogenarian. If the present owner of this house were eighty-five, his daughter, in her fifties or sixties, would have written for him."

All at once Mr. Maltby frowned at himself. The frown was followed by an apologetic shrug.

"You must forgive me for these apparent diversions," he said. "Actually, they are not diversions at all. I am thinking aloud.

Trying to recreate, as far as I can, the atmosphere and circumstances of this house when Charles got up this morning. When you find the atmosphere, facts resolve themselves inside it. You hear the thunder before it comes. Storm-clouds—a sudden unnatural flutter of still leaves—a cat chasing its tail——"

He jumped to his feet. Mr. Hopkins went back in his chair as though he had been shot. David remained still, but with a distressing tightening of his forehead.

"I see Charles!" cried the old man. "I see him! Not his face! His soul! Here he comes—down the stairs—yes, there's his face, now—pale, deadly pale—a man with a sick spirit—terrified—the picture—are you looking at it, Charles?——"

He stopped speaking. He returned quietly to his chair.

"Now for this afternoon."

"No, wait a moment!" gasped Mr. Hopkins.

"What for?" asked Mr. Maltby.

"I—I don't know. Yes, I do. Do you think it would be—I mean to say—was there any whisky in the stores?"

"You can go and see."

"Yes!" He rose, but sat down again. "No, after all. Carry on, carry on." His hand moved towards his handkerchief, but again he did not complete an operation he had begun, and the hand returned limply to his knee, as though ashamed of itself. "Of course," he said with the travesty of a grin, "you didn't *really* see—er—Charles, did you?"

"Clearly enough," answered Mr. Maltby.

"Yes, exactly," murmured Mr. Hopkins, without any idea what he meant.

Then he forgot his shame, and indulged in another thorough mopping.

"May I interrupt with a question?" asked David.

"Of course," replied the old man.

"I'm not sure whether it's appropriate to the point we've reached, but—that room. The one you warned Smith not to enter. Did you see anybody there?"

Mr. Maltby smiled.

"I can answer that more definitely. I am afraid I created that bedroom out of my imagination, and also the alleged menace inside it, although I admit that inventing menaces in this house is like carrying coals to Newcastle. My object was to reduce Smith's taste for wandering about loose, for the reasons I have already given."

"Thank you. Now I'll try and be quiet."

"I don't want you to. I am telling you a story, and your duty is to search for its flaws. Well, to proceed, we come now to this afternoon. Charles, having controlled any qualms he may have had, lights the fires in the hall, the drawing-room, this dining-room, the kitchen—no, that was assumedly lit before—and two bedrooms. I understand from Miss Carrington that the fire in Mr. Thomson's room—Charles's room—was laid but not lit, and that she lit that herself when Mr. Thomson was put there."

"Quite correct," answered David. "I have wood and coal in Thomson's room down on my list."

"Why not add the match?" murmured Mr. Hopkins.

"That done, Charles waits," went on Mr. Maltby; "and his master and the daughter arrive."

"I think I've spotted a flaw here, sir," said David.

"Let me have it."

"When did they arrive?"

"I place it this afternoon. You will remember, tea was pre-pared for them."

"Yes, but according to your interpretation of the letter—if that's correct—they were not due to arrive till the evening, just before dinner."

"I agree there seems something wrong with our pattern here," nodded Mr. Maltby, "yet it also seems too much of a coincidence to suppose that two other people should have arrived. Don't you think so?"

"They might have been visitors," proposed Mr. Hopkins.

"Visitors, in this weather?" queried Mr. Maltby. "Besides, is it likely that Charles would invite visitors just before his master's arrival? Certainly this is not the kind of weather in which visi-tors just drop in for a chat."

"I've thought of one more point," said David.

"What?"

"The cups. There were three. Would Charles have tea with the others?"

"That is a very good point. I am not sure that I can deal with it." The old man frowned, and stared almost accusingly at Exhibit C. "Yes, yes, there are one or two things here——" He threw up his hands. "Your point beats me for the moment, Mr. Carrington. Some trivial detail might adjust it. We must remem-ber it, while proceeding with what, after all, remains the more likely hypothesis—namely, that the people for whom that tea was prepared were the people who were expected. The owner of the house and his daughter. Perhaps—yes, perhaps they altered their plans and arrived earlier than originally intended because of the weather."

"The weather would have made 'em arrive later," argued Mr. Hopkins.

"If they had not advanced their plans on account of it," retorted Mr. Maltby. "That is exactly what I am now suggesting."

"Quite so, quite so," murmured Mr. Hopkins. "I'm only trying to help."

"The weakness remains, however. I'm not satisfied, but for the moment this appears to be the best we can arrive at. The master and the daughter arrive before tea. How long before tea? Not long.... The devil knows how they got here——"

"Perhaps they *did* arrive long before tea, Mr. Maltby," interposed David, "and got here before the weather worked up to its present pitch."

"In that case, why do not the bedrooms show it? They would go to their rooms if they arrived long before tea, but if they arrived just before they might wait for the needed cup before ascending."

"And leave their luggage below," answered David. "Where's the luggage?"

"Yes, I was just going to ask that," exclaimed Mr. Hopkins, annoyed that he had been too late with the question. "They wouldn't turn up for a week with only a toothpick!"

"I have also asked myself that question, and as yet I have no answer to it," admitted Mr. Maltby. "If they arrived by car or some other conveyance, they would undoubtedly bring their luggage with them. But, how about this? They could not get a car to bring them from whatever station they arrived at. Presumably

Hemmersby, some five miles distant. They decided, therefore, to leave the luggage behind, and send for it later. They certainly took no luggage away with them."

"How do you know that?"

"You shall hear in a minute. The trouble is that we have no inkling of *why* they came. Their motive. I doubt whether it was just to enjoy Christmas here. I believe they came for some special purpose—a purpose that worried Charles Shaw considerably. Yes, if we knew why they came we might understand more about the manner of their coming, and their going.

"Still—they came. They came while we were chatting in the train, and while Smith was killing Barling in the next compartment. They came—and, very swiftly, something happened."

Mr. Maltby paused, and his eyes now travelled to Exhibit A, the hammer. Mr. Hopkins tried to prevent his eyes from following the example.

"We do not know what the something was. We have got to find that out. We do not know whether the situation that arose was spontaneous or premeditated. If the ghost of that old man hanging on the wall had a voice, I'll wager it could tell us. Maybe presently it will! But we do know the sequel. Three people were in this house, and three people left it. Two of the three were alive."

He corrected himself.

"No, I am wrong. All three were alive, in all probability, unless the third died indoors and was taken out afterwards by the other two. I doubt that, however, from our present evidence, which suggests that all three left the house, but one did not get far.

"Listen. I've told you that I followed Smith and lost him. I have also told you that I found him again just before we both entered the house—myself for the first time, Smith for the second. But I have not told you what happened to me between the losing and the finding of Smith.

"After he had vanished I was able to follow his tracks for a while as, later, you doubtless followed mine. Then I lost the tracks, and floundered about in a hopeless maze. A most unpleasant period. I hope I never have to endure another like it. But I must have floundered somewhere in this district, as I am convinced I was not far from this house when I suddenly saw a figure a little way ahead of me.

"I thought it was Smith, and increased my pace, but when the figure was joined by another figure—it seemed to come out of nowhere—I realised my error. The second figure, though I only got a very blurred sight of it, was a woman."

"The daughter?" asked Mr. Hopkins.

"If our original surmise is correct, the daughter," answered Mr. Maltby, "but whether the man was Charles Shaw or his master I cannot say. You will realise the importance of the identity.

"They were hurrying, to put it mildly. I tried hard to overtake them, but they soon melted out of my sight. Then I found the hammer.

"It was obvious that it had been recently dropped. The inference was that one of those two scurrying figures had dropped it. I was as sure that they were flying from fear as I had been that Smith was flying from fear. I began a final effort to catch them up, putting the hammer in my pocket as I did so. Then I tripped over something that I thought was a log. Went headlong over it, and rolled down a bank. When I picked myself up I did not know whether I was facing north, south, east or west. If your snow in Dawson City was worse than this, Mr. Hopkins, may I never be in Dawson City. I was temporarily blinded.

"But I expect Fate was looking after me. It still had a use for me, and it is only when that use concludes that we can write 'Finis' to our lives. I wandered round and round in a circle for perhaps ten minutes. That's a guess. I was as confused as to time as I was to direction, but it must have been long enough for Smith to reach the house—he just missed the other fugitives—for you to reach the house after Smith, and for Smith to make his first get-away through the attic window, because it was Smith who brought me back to solid matters. We nearly ran into each other. And beyond Smith I saw a more welcome solid matter. This house.

"What happened after that, you both know."

"Yes, but look here, why didn't you go back and look for that—that log!" demanded Mr. Hopkins, as Mr. Maltby paused.

"I had wandered around for ten minutes without coming upon it again," answered Mr. Maltby. "I had no idea where to look. Besides, at that time I thought it *was* a log. I had not then found hairs upon the hammer."

"Whew!" muttered Mr. Hopkins.

"But do not imagine I am justifying, much less glorifying, my conduct outside this house," said Mr. Maltby. "It is human to err, and I am definitely human. Particularly after a tumble. At my age, one is not good in snowstorms."

"Well, sir, I must go out and find that—log, now!" exclaimed David, rising.

"Certainly—if you can," replied Mr. Maltby acidly. "It's a nice sunny night."

The next moment Mr. Hopkins sprang to his feet, while his eyes looked ready to shoot from his head.

From the hall sounded faltering footsteps, and a hollow voice droning, "*Here it comes, here it comes ... crash!*"

CHAPTER XV

FIGHTING THE TIDE

"You're not eating your pineapple," said Lydia.

"No, somehow I can't," answered Jessie. "I mean, I'm not hungry."

"The first idea was right," replied Lydia. "You mean you can't!"

She walked to the window, drew the curtain aside a little, and stared out, while Jessie watched her back.

"That's right, I can't," said Jessie. "I suppose it's still snowing?"

"It doesn't look as if it's ever going to stop. Where on earth does it all come from?"

Outside the window-pane the floating snowflakes showed no sign of having spent themselves.

"Why are you staying up here?" asked Jessie suddenly.

"Don't you want me to?" answered Lydia, turning.

"Of course, you know I do; only that's not the reason you're staying. What are they doing downstairs?"

"Oh, just chatting."

"What about?"

"I don't know."

"Well, you don't think they're telling funny stories, do you? Something's happened! Please tell me! I heard that scream!"

"Scream?"

"Yes, what was it?"

"I don't know what it was, Miss Noyes, and you can believe me this time. Let's talk about something else."

"All right. Who's your favourite film star? Mine's Gary Cooper."

Lydia smiled. "I admit it's difficult," she said, "but we'll keep on trying. Did you see him in 'Mr. Deeds'?"

"Miss Carrington, it's no *good*!" retorted Jessie doggedly. "If you say you don't know what that scream was I believe you, but something has happened downstairs and that's why you're staying with me, I can tell by your attitude. No one's been hurt, have they? Your brother's all right, isn't he? And, of course, the others?"

Then Lydia gave up.

"You win," she answered. "My brother is quite all right, but something did happen. Mr. Hopkins and Smith had a row, and—and Smith's gone."

"Gone!"

"Yes."

"Well, I don't expect anybody minds that much, but why did he go?"

"Because of the row——"

"Oh, dear, you *won't* tell me! What was the row about?"

"You remember that—trouble on the train?"

"What Mr. Hopkins told us about?"

"Yes, well he accused Smith, and Smith went for him, but when the others joined in he scooted. That, without frills, is the story."

Jessie remained silent for awhile, absorbing the story. Then she whispered:

"Does that mean—it was true?"

"Seems rather like it," replied Lydia. "Anyhow, he's gone now, so we needn't worry."

She did not mention that he had taken a knife with him.

"Suppose he comes back?"

"I don't imagine he will."

"No.... Was it he who screamed?"

"I don't know."

"Did any one go after him?"

"I don't know. I mean no, no one did. That would be too ridiculous! Look here, Miss Noyes, let's pretend, if only for fifteen minutes, that everything's all right, that we're in a lovely old house—and it *is* a lovely old house—look at this room, it's the sort I've dreamed about—and that the only ghost in it is a dear old lady who had a wonderful romance here when she was a girl, and who likes to return sometimes to remember it.... You don't *really* believe in ghosts, do you? Really and truly, and no spoof?"

"No. Yes. I don't know," replied Jessie, striving to be truthful.

"Nonsense, of course you don't. They're just imagination, and therefore we can imagine them as we like. So mine's the dear old lady—can't you see her?—she's in lavender, of course, and she has a lace cap—has she?—yes, a lace cap, and mittens, and very bright eyes, that are somehow young in spite of her wrinkles. And yours—what can your ghost be? I know, the great-great-grandfather of Gary Cooper, who was born here, and who used to stand at that window wondering whether he'd ever have a famous great-great-grandson."

Jessie smiled, as nonsense advanced on apprehension.

"I think you're extraordinary, the way you take things," she said. "I wish I could."

"Of course you can!" retorted Lydia. "As a matter of fact, you do. Go on about your ghost."

"I wouldn't know how to."

"Do your bit!"

"All right. My ghost meets your ghost. Then what happens?"

"A lot of little ghosts. Oh, my goodness, I'm going dippy, but if you're going dippy anyhow you might as well choose a pleasant way. If a lot of little ghosts *would* be pleasant? Imagine them running about all over the house, dodging under beds and hiding round corners and scampering up and down the stairs!"

"I think they'd be rather fun."

"Then we'll have 'em at the Christmas feast to-morrow. You haven't forgotten to-morrow's Christmas, have you?" She glanced at her wrist-watch. "In three hours and forty-four minutes. Soon be time to hang up the stocking! I remember one Christmas—it was about seven years ago——"

She began to reminisce. She made it a very long one. Only half of it was true, for whenever she found Jessie's attention wandering she brought her interest back with blatant fabrications. She felt as though she were swimming against a strong dark tide, and that once she stopped swimming the tide would get her and carry her to places she was trying to avoid. One of the places was not very far beyond the window, at the unknown spot from which the cry had come.

At last her inventive faculty gave out. She had kept the one-sided conversation going for a quarter of an hour, and suddenly she realised that she was no longer getting any assistance from her audience. She became conscious of Jessie's utter silence, as well as of the utter silence of the house, and her fighting spirit began to ooze away.... What *was* happening down below? Why didn't some one come up and tell her? David had promised not to keep her in the dark.... Yes, and what was happening to Jessie? She was not merely silent, she was staring. Not at anything in particular. Just staring....

"What's the matter?" asked Lydia sharply.

Jessie did not reply before the question had been repeated. Then she wrenched her focus back from infinity to normal, and answered:

"Nothing."

"A little while ago you wanted *me* to tell the truth, and I told it to you," said Lydia.

"Yes, but I don't know whether it *was*—anything," murmured Jessie, with a shudder.

"Well, what did it seem to be? You look as pale as a——" She pulled herself up and altered the simile from "ghost" to "—sheet. And you haven't said a single word for at least five minutes! Have you heard what I've been talking about?"

"Yes."

"Repeat my last sentence?"

"Well, I did miss that."

"I said, 'And Where do you think they found my shoe? In the soup tureen.'"

"Oh, *that* was where it was?"

"What was?"

"What do you mean? Your shoe."

"What shoe?"

"The one you were telling me about."

"I wasn't telling you about any shoe, I was telling you about the time I swallowed the sixpence out of the Christmas pudding, so you see you didn't only miss the last sentence, you missed the whole story. You haven't heard a word. And I'm asking you why?"

Jessie took a breath.

"Of course, you'd draw the heart out of a lettuce! I—I expect it was this—this bed."

"Bed?" repeated Lydia. "What about the bed?"

"I don't know," replied Jessie. "I dare say it's all my imagination."

"Miss Noyes, do you want me to shake you?"

"All right, I'll tell you, at least I'll try, but I really don't know how to explain it. It's—a feeling I get. I've had it before. Once, when you were out of the room."

"What sort of a feeling?"

"That's what I mean, it's almost impossible to put it into words without it seeming just silly. First I'm frightened—there you are, it sounds silly at once——"

"It isn't silly to be frightened in this house," Lydia interposed. "You're not the only one."

"Yes, but this isn't just the ordinary kind of fear. It's—I don't know—I seem to be afraid of something special even though I don't know what it is. And the bed seems to be holding me in it—to be pressing me down. And then I think some one's coming—isn't it idiotic?—I expect it's really imagination. Yes!" she exclaimed. "Now I come to think of it, it probably was, because I feel a sort of pain in my stomach, I began to get it when you brought me the pineapple."

"Was that why you didn't eat it?" asked Lydia.

"Oh, no. At least, I don't think so. No, I'm sure not. You see, that wasn't one of the times—I mean, I only began to get it then, and then it went away again.... Well, now you *know* I can't explain it!" And then, all at once, she gave an exclamation that conveyed more than any of her struggling words. "This bed's ghastly!"

"Then why have you stayed in it?" demanded Lydia. "You'd better get out of it now—I'll help you to a chair!"

Jessie frowned.

"But—Miss Carrington—it can't *really* be anything, can it?" she asked.

"It doesn't matter whether it is or isn't——"

"Yes, it does matter! I mean, to me, it does. There's nothing I can't stand more than being frightened—you aren't for instance—and so I'll never let myself be. I mean, pay any attention to it, what's the good? When I'm nervous, even on First Nights, which are nothing really, I mean the part I play in them, I say, 'Don't be a goose.' If I don't, I go to bits. You can't help being as you are, and anyhow, that's how I'm made."

"The way you're made seems a very good way to me, Miss Noyes," answered Lydia, "but whether what you feel about that bed is imagination or not, I'm going to get you out of it—because that's how *I'm* made!"

There was a large, soft arm-chair in the room. A minute later Jessie was settled in it, with her foot on a stool, and the bed-spread over her. Lydia assisted in the moving operation, though Jessie declared that her foot was getting better.

"You help everybody, don't you?" said Jessie, in a mood to be over-sentimental.

"Not so I notice it," answered Lydia. "There's somebody I haven't helped lately, at any rate, and that's Mr. Thomson. Will you be all right if I leave you for a moment to go and have a look at him?"

"Of course," replied Jessie.

Lydia ran out of the room. She did not know why she ran, or why she felt so suddenly restless. Of course, there could not really be any significance in Jessie's strange sensations in the bed....

Thomson's door was a little way along the passage on the opposite side. She knocked. Receiving no answer, she opened the door and looked in. Thomson's bed was empty, and the bedclothes were strewn all over the floor.

CHAPTER XVI

THE IMAGINATION OF ROBERT THOMSON

EVEN with a normal temperature Robert Thomson lived largely in his imagination, using it to redress the shortcomings of reality or to repair its ravages. His external life made only a faint impression on him because it was so boring and uneventful, and while he filled ledgers with meaningless figures and assured clients of his firm's best attention, or else listened to his aunt's tedious self-pitying conversation, his mind was busy with its compensating work, either glorifying the commonplace or escaping from it altogether.

Sometimes, while writing in his ledgers, Thomson recreated himself as a potential genius rising from the bottom of the rung to the top—"Nobody imagined that Sir Robert, then an unknown young man working in a basement office, would one day be First Lord of the Admiralty"—or while listening to his aunt he became Good Samaritan No. One, watched approvingly by God Himself. More often, however, he chose the path of complete escape, where his exploits were simpler and more stirringly human. He did not ache most for the cold prizes of fame; he wanted the appreciation and affection of those around him. So he walked in sweet intimacy with beautiful women, or served them after aerial accidents. He could rescue a child who had fallen over the cliffs of Beachy Head while answering a telephone. But the aerial accidents were his chief delight.

All this with a normal temperature. When the temperature rose above normal, soaring beyond the hundred, his imagination took complete charge. Always within easy call, it had but a short journey to the controls, and it used them swiftly and with a ruthless grotesqueness. "You want some fun?" it jeered to the fevered brain. "By heck, you shall have it!" Only, of course, it was not always fun.

Thomson's imagination had taken complete charge of him shortly, though not quite immediately, after Lydia conducted him up to his bedroom. The fact that a beautiful girl had performed this service gave an added fillip to his temperature. When the door had closed and he had found himself alone on a strange bed, he relaxed at first into a kind of peaceful coma rich with scents and colours. Closing his eyes, he discovered a magic kaleidoscope that shifted its varying hues gloriously and always resolved into one particular face. Even when he opened his eyes the colours and the face remained, though they were disturbed by other outlines—the end of a bed, the back of a chair, a slightly moving curtain (it seemed to move, whether it did or not), pyjamas hanging from a hook. Such things as these tried to wrest him back to actualities from his inarticulate orgy.

One incident occurred of which no one in the house ever knew but himself. He only remembered it dimly. It occurred during the last period before imagination captured him utterly—a period when he was jerked back from semi-consciousness for his final wrestle with solid facts. The fact that stood out pre-eminently was his loneliness.

The loneliness was unbearable. To lie here on this bed was to drop out of the adventure. It suggested impotence, when he wanted to be useful. It gave him ghostly solitude, when he needed human companionship. It took him "out of things."

"I'm not going to stay here!" he muttered. "I'm all right—just a bit hot—but all right. I'm going down again!"

He sat up. The outlines wobbled. He turned the sheets back. The sheets wobbled, as did the hand that turned them. He put a foot out of bed.

Somehow or other he left the bed, and somehow or other he managed to crawl half-way to the door. Then he stopped, and space rushed at him. He tried to grip supports that were not there. The floor rose. He found himself flat upon it. Somehow or other, he crawled back to bed....

"What made you so late?" asked his aunt.

They were riding from the station to her house on a couple of elephants.

"The snow," answered Thomson.

"People have always got excuses when they're not kind to me," retorted his aunt.

"But it really was the snow," replied Thomson. "The train got held up."

"There's been no snow here. Look, it's sunny. I don't leave any money to people who aren't kind to me."

"You don't think I visit you because of your money, do you?"

"Of course, that's the reason. It's everybody's reason. You think I don't know what's going on in your mind all the time, but I do. You're never really interested in me, and you're scared stiff that I'll find it out, well, I have found it out, and now you shan't have anything. I shall leave it all to my elephants."

They reached the house and dismounted. The elephants went into two large kennels. As his aunt took a big key from her pocket she said:

"I was going to give you twenty thousand pounds for Christmas, but now you shall only have a tie. You could have married on twenty thousand pounds. Do you know how late you are? A week. It's next year. What'll they say to you at the office?"

She opened the door, and he walked into his office. His aunt turned into his boss, who scowled at him.

"What made you so late?" demanded his boss.

"The snow, sir," answered Thomson.

"Well, don't let it happen again," snapped his boss. "If it does, you'll be sacked. The auditors are coming. Suppose you haven't got your books done before they come? What'll happen? They'll murder us all."

Thomson walked to his desk. It was a kitchen table. He opened the drawer in which he kept the bread-knife for sharpening his pencil. There was no bread-knife.

"There you are!" shouted his boss behind him. "The auditors have taken it! Hurry!"

A big pile of books was on the table. He had to get through them all, otherwise he would receive the bread-knife in his back. He opened the first one, and began adding figures: "Seven, nine, sixteen, twenty-three, four, eight, thirty-two, forty-one——" But when he wanted to jot down the total, he found that his pencil had no point! And the auditors had his bread-knife!

He ran round the room, trying to find another pencil. He searched everywhere. In cups, tea-pots, railway carriages, elephant-kennels. He must find a pencil before the auditors came! Returning at last to the kitchen table, he dipped his finger desperately in a bottle of ink, and tried to write the total by using his nail as a nib. The result was a blot. The blot grew larger and larger, till it covered the whole sheet. Bathed in perspiration—the room was like an oven—he tore the page out and threw it into a waste-paper basket.

"I'll be all right," he thought, "so long as they don't look in the waste-paper basket."

Then the door opened. He kept very still. He knew it was an auditor, and he did not want to be seen. He had not written down the total yet. The figures were swimming before his hot eyes. If only the auditor would go—give him just a little more time—he was sure he could do it.

But the auditor did not go. He was an old man, and he was creeping round the room. He was getting nearer and nearer to the waste-paper basket. Thomson dared not look at him, but he heard him dive down, and he knew the withered hand had taken the paper out of the waste-paper basket.

"He's found it," gasped Thomson. "Now for the bread-knife. Well, anyhow, I won't need my aunt's money now."

The old man left the waste-paper basket, and bent over Thomson. It was Mr. Maltby, but Thomson did not know that. Everything went black.

The blackness dissolved. Now another face was peering at him. It was a wonderful face, a face he had known years ago, when life was smiling. Again Thomson did not know it was Lydia's face. The face melted away while he strove to retain it. It melted into the blackness from which it had come, and he took a long journey through a dark tunnel trying to find it again. The tunnel was dotted with little specks of white. Flying, whirling, blinding, choking. He ran fast. He stopped running. Somewhere in that whirling confusion a person had screamed....

Now he ran again. He ran back to the table and the ledgers. The pile had grown a mile in height, but as he looked upwards, becoming smaller and smaller as the pile grew taller and taller, he made a tremendous effort to escape from the dark world of oppressions that was trying to stamp him out. He knew there was something that could save him—one thing—if only he could remember it. What was it? What was it? What was it? If the kitchen fire with the boiling kettle had not been quite so hot, he could have thought of it at once. What was it?

Then, suddenly, he found it. He was looking in the right direction. Far, far above the tall pile of ledgers was a little moving dot. A tiny light, like a star skimming through the black sky. An aeroplane.

He rose. Bedclothes sprayed from him. He became entangled in them, escaped from them, fled from their retaining grasp, and knocked over a small table. He had found his star, and he must follow it, because he knew what would happen when it crashed. She would be in it—she who had worn a thousand different faces, but whose heart was always the same. She was up there in that swiftly moving, swiftly falling star. And when she crashed (she would not be hurt—she never was) he would be on the spot to help her from the burning aeroplane, and to carry her to a cottage, and to receive her thanks, and her understanding, and the oblivion she always brought....

"Gently with him," said Mr. Maltby, from the dining-room doorway. "I think we'd better get him to the settee in the drawing-room for the moment. And let Miss Carrington know."

CHAPTER XVII

REFLECTIONS OF THE PAST

BUT Lydia did not need telling; she already knew. After finding Thomson's bedroom empty, she had returned to the top of the stairs just as the delirious man had crumpled into David's arms at the bottom, and now she came flying down. "It's a miracle only one of us is off his head!" she gasped, half-hysterically. "I'm not guaranteeing how much longer *I'll* last!"

Fortunately Thomson gave them no trouble. His babbling ceased, and they quickly got him to his new quarters on the drawing-room couch. The bedclothes with which he had wrestled were brought down, and Lydia placed them over him again. But when it was suggested that he should not be left alone and that she should act as night nurse, she hesitated.

"I'm game to do whatever's best," she said, "but can I be spared for the job? I've got some one else to look after, you know—Miss Noyes."

"She is nervous upstairs?" queried Mr. Maltby.

"Who wouldn't be?" she answered. "I've had to get *her* out of bed, too!"

"Why's that?" exclaimed David in surprise.

"Don't ask me, my dear! She's the one to tell you. My own explanation would just be the bald one that the bed is haunted."

"Eh? Haunted?" cried Mr. Hopkins.

"Yes, haunted," responded Lydia. "The bed gives her strange feelings and pains in her stomach, so I've stuck her in an arm-chair. What's going to be the next? Ours is a nice house, ours is!"

Mr. Maltby looked thoughtful. They were standing in the hall, and his eyes moved towards the watchful old gentleman on the wall over the fireplace. David received a queer impression that a live old man was asking a mute question of a dead one.

"What is she doing now?" Mr. Maltby inquired.

"Waiting for me," answered Lydia.

"Then you'd better go up to her."

"And what are *you* going to do? About *him*?" She nodded towards the drawing-room door, which was ajar. "And—other things?"

"*I'm* going to see about the other things," replied David grimly.

"You're not going out?"

"Got to. If I can. Just a little way."

"Expect you're right, but for God's sake be careful!"

"Don't worry."

"Better wait until we know how Miss Noyes is," advised Mr. Maltby, and added as Lydia turned to mount the stairs: "Is it only the bed?"

"You mean, that's—worrying her?"

"Yes."

"She hasn't mentioned anything else."

"Nothing about the room itself?"

"No. But——"

"What?"

"She's a funny little thing. All nerves and no admission. She doesn't admit her nerves till you drag things out of her. I had to drag this."

"Yes—she's sensitive. I wonder whether it wouldn't be better to have her down here?"

"Much better," agreed Mr. Hopkins, "if we're going to sit up all night."

"Oh, then you don't think of returning to your own room?" asked Mr. Maltby dryly.

"Eh? Well, the way things are working out, it might be a good idea if we all stick together. More companionable, you know. Knowing where we all are."

"Well, see how Miss Noyes feels about it, will you, Miss Carrington?" said Mr. Maltby.

"I'll come up and lend a hand if she wants to return to the happy family," added David.

"Right, I'll tell her," replied Lydia. "But she may not need your help this time, her foot's improving."

She vanished up the stairs.

"Interesting about that bed," murmured Mr. Maltby.

David moved to the drawing-room door and poked his head in. Thomson was lying quietly on the couch, his form flickering in the firelight. None of the fires had been allowed to die down. They were the warm spots in a house of chills.

"Is he all right?" asked Mr. Hopkins, as David turned back to the hall.

"O.K.," replied David.

"We owe him one for the shock he gave us," said Mr. Hopkins. "What did he mean about that crash?"

"A delirious person never means anything," returned David.

"On the contrary, Mr. Carrington, a delirious man always means something," remarked Mr. Maltby, "but the meaning is usually obscure. Nothing in existence is without a meaning, or a result. If you dream that you are punting on the Amazon with a toothpick, the dream will have both a reason and a consequence, though you may never become conscious of either."

"The one thing I have learned in this house, Mr. Maltby," answered David, "is never to argue with you. Hallo, here comes Lydia. Well, what news from the first floor front? Reinforcements wanted?"

"Yes, please," responded Lydia from the stairs. "We held a lightning conference, and we decided to retreat to the base!"

David found Jessie standing on one foot by her chair. She was trying to prove how much better she was, and she declared that she no longer needed to be carried. He waved her objections aside, however, lifted her small weight in his arms, and carried her down to the dining-room, depositing her in a chair near the door.

"What's the matter?" he exclaimed suddenly.

She appeared on the verge of collapse.

"I—I don't know!" she gasped. "Please! Somewhere else!"

Without understanding he complied quickly, helping her to another chair, and waiting for the explanation that did not come. She just sat and panted.

"Good Lord, I've hurt her!" he murmured with anxious penitence.

She did not seem to hear him. Her eyes were closed.

"Let her alone," came Mr. Maltby's abrupt voice. "Don't worry her! I'll deal with this."

He had been standing by the chair Jessie had just left, regarding it fixedly. It was a chair that had not previously been used. Unlike the rest, it had slender wooden arms.

Now, all at once, he darted to the table. Jessie's eyes were still closed, and she did not see the object he was bringing towards her. But the others saw it. It was Exhibit A. The hammer.

While Lydia stared at it—she had not seen it before, and knew nothing of its significance—and while Mr. Hopkins fell back upon the chronic necessity of mopping his forehead with his handkerchief, David fought an impulse to rush at the old man and seize the hammer from his hands. He said afterwards that, at this moment, he felt almost murderous himself; not because he distrusted Mr. Maltby, but because the idea of Death had suddenly filled the air, making it nauseating and stifling. He could not bear the thought that the hammer was on its way towards Jessie's closed eyes.

He did not move, however. Something held him motionless. He remained rooted to his spot even when Mr. Maltby raised the hammer slowly, and slowly touched Jessie's forehead with it.

Her eyes opened. The pupils dilated with unspeakable horror. Then something snapped within David, and he leapt forward. As he did so, the old man retreated a pace, and brought the hammer quickly behind his back.

Mr. Maltby's eyes never left Jessie's. It was that invisible line of contact that stopped David's onrush. He felt that if he had passed through it he would have been scorched.

"What was it?" asked Mr. Maltby quietly.

"A hammer," came Jessie's response. Her voice was flat and toneless.

"What happened?"

"It hit me?"

"Did it hurt?"

"Yes."

"What do you feel?"

"Nothing."

"Nothing at all?"

"Nothing at all."

"You are asleep?"

"Yes."

"Sleep."

"Sleep."

Her eyes closed again....

When she reopened them she was on the couch in the hall. She raised her head and looked around muzzily.

"Where——?" she murmured. "I—thought—"

Lydia, seated on a stool near her feet, quickly banished an anxious expression and smiled at her reassuringly. A little way off, the rather flabby form of Mr. Hopkins lolled limply in a chair. He was dozing fitfully, emitting tiny snores. Mr. Maltby was by the drawing-room door, listening.

"What's happening?" asked Jessie.

"Nothing," replied Lydia. "Go to sleep again."

"Yes—but wasn't I—didn't he carry me into the dining-room?"

"You remember that?"

It was Mr. Maltby's question. He left the drawing-room door as he spoke and approached the couch.

"Yes."

"And then?"

"Where is he?"

"What do you remember after Mr. Carrington took you into the dining-room?"

Lydia noticed that Mr. Maltby's voice was very different now from the voice he had used in his previous interrogation of Jessie. It was no longer a compelling monotone—it was human and encouraging.

"I'm not sure," replied Jessie. "My head aches. Yes, I remember. He——" She stopped suddenly. "He put me in a chair," she whispered.

The hall clock began striking. She counted the chimes.

"Eleven!" she exclaimed, surprised. "Have I been asleep an hour? I—I expect I—dreamt it."

"Can we hear the dream?" asked Mr. Maltby.

"But I only remember a little more—and I'd rather not remember it," she answered.

"Why not? Didn't you like the chair?"

"How did you know that?"

"Well, you said you'd rather not remember it."

"Of course, so I did. No, it was horrible. I couldn't stay in it."

"In what way, horrible?"

"I can't possibly describe what I felt like."

"Angry?"

"Angry? No! Nothing like that."

"Jealous?"

"No."

"As though—you'd been hit?"

"No. What makes you say that?"

"Dizzy? Sick? Breathless——"

"Yes!" she exclaimed. "Breathless!"

"Pain anywhere? Dull? Sharp? Heart thumping——"

"No, no; just the opposite! I remember now—there was a pain, and I thought my heart had stopped." She added, "It's thumping now, though!"

Lydia glanced at Mr. Maltby.

"Let's postpone this cross-examination," she suggested. "I think she's been through enough!"

"There is just one more question I want to ask," replied the old man, and turned back to Jessie. "You thought, for an instant, that your heart had stopped. In that case you would have been dead."

"It felt like that!"

"But *you* are not dead, so you need not worry on that score. Were your sensations similar to your sensations in the four-poster bed?"

Jessie looked at him wide-eyed.

"Yes! No! I mean, I don't know! It was—the same pain!" She shuddered. "Please, I don't want to talk about it. Let's talk about other things. How's poor Mr. Thomson? Has he done any more sleep-walking?"

"He's sleeping, but not walking, in the drawing-room," replied Lydia.

"And Mr. Carrington?" As no one answered her, she repeated the question sharply. "Where is he? Is he all right?"

"He's just having a look round," said Lydia. "He'll be back in a few minutes."

For Jessie's peace of mind, she did not add that David's look around had so far lasted three-quarters of an hour.

CHAPTER XVIII
WHAT HAPPENED TO DAVID

WHEN David left the house by the back window through which Smith had preceded him, to begin his overdue search for the cause of the murderers's scream—both the front and the back doors were blocked, but the mounting snow had only just reached the level of the window-ledge and it was possible to clamber out on to a white slope—he found to his relief that the flakes were descending a little less thickly. This was the one crumb of consolation in the unsavoury but necessary journey.

He rolled down the slope at an uncomfortable pace, and his first job on reaching the bottom was to pick himself up and to expel the mouthfuls he had taken during the roll. Then he looked about him for a clue to his next direction.

Two sets of footprints grew dimly into his vision as he lowered his head to peer at the snow. This was *embarras de richesses*. One set continued straight on, towards trees; the other curved round to the right. He chose the latter because the prints were more distinct, and had therefore, assumedly, been more recently made.

They led him a zigzag dance, almost as though they were trying to shake him off. First they slanted back towards the house, but when they reached the bank of snow that obscured three-quarters of the back door they turned away abruptly for about ten yards, and then turned back again. After that they zigzagged confusedly and uncertainly, suggesting that the person who had made them had been in a doubtful or furtive mood.

Suddenly David gained an impression that something was wrong somewhere, and after peering at the prints more closely he found out what was wrong and called himself every name under the sun. The toe-marks were not pointing ahead of him but towards him.

"Blithering idiot!" he thought. "I'm tracing this trip the wrong way—backwards!"

He paused to work it out. Did he want to find out where the person had come from? That might be interesting, but it was more important to find out where the person had gone to. Wherever he had come from, he had evidently made a tour round most of the house, reaching eventually the vicinity of the back door. And then?

Were the other tracks—the tracks leading straight to the trees—a continuation of the journey?

"Can't be," reflected David. "Those other tracks were made first!"

He tried again.

"How about this? I'm not on Smith's track at all. Smith made the track towards the trees. The person who made the track I am now on is some other person who came along a little while after Smith's flight. Why did he come along? Did he hear that scream? And then did he creep out from wherever he was hiding, sneak round the house, and try to see or hear something through the windows or doors?"

It was not a pleasant theory. If the person were the man or woman Mr. Maltby had seen flying from the house before tea, one of whom had lost the sinister Exhibit A, the eavesdropper might have overheard some personal news!

"Yes, but would they still be hanging around here after all this time?" he wondered. "Wouldn't they get clear as soon as they jolly well could? And why only one of them—why not both?" He gazed at the single track of prints. "They might have been looking for each other—or for the hammer—or they might have returned for something they needed in the house!"

The last idea pulled him up sharply. He recalled that he had left the back window open, and that if the track to the trees had not been made by the person who had sneaked round the house, he had come upon no other evidence of any continuation of that person's journey.... The person might have been lurking near by, concealed, while David was rolling down the snowbank—waiting.

Quickly he retraced his way, no longer following the trail's irregularities but making as directly as he could for his original starting point. When he reached the spot his anxiety was set at rest. The slope of snow down which he had rolled bore no fresh marks, and the obvious assumption was that no one had ascended it during his absence. But as he turned from this welcome discovery to look at the track towards the trees, a fresh shock awaited him. Beside the fading footprints was a second set. They were clear and well defined, and had not been there five minutes ago!

His mind worked rapidly, in response to this startling new development. He was convinced now that somebody *had* watched him roll down the snow bank, and had waited till he had vanished round the house before continuing an interrupted journey.

Well, now he had to continue his own journey, and without any particular relish for the job he made for the trees.

"This is the way Smith went," he thought, ploughing through the deep snow that seemed to be trying to hold back his feet as they sank into its soft grip, "and soon I shall reach the spot where Smith screamed!"

He reached it in two minutes. If he had not been warned he might have passed it by, but Mr. Maltby had planted a picture in his mind that made it impossible for him to miss the original, and he recognised the grim mound as soon as he saw it. It was just beyond the first fringe of white-clothed trees, a little to the side of a narrow lane that wound between them.

He stared at the mound, gleaming gloomily at him like a pale grave, and felt slightly sick. Was there really some one beneath that significant shape of snow, and was it really his duty to dig that some one out? Now it had come to the point, he wondered just exactly where his duty lay, and what service he would perform by exposing the tragedy. The form beneath the snow was lifeless. Where could he take it if he uncovered it? To the house to add to the existing horrors there? He doubted whether, in any case, he had the strength to carry the burden. Yet to uncover it, and to leave it where it was, would merely be to give it back to the snow again.

Suddenly he decided on another course. He did not know whether he was choosing simply the easier or the better path, and he refused to explore that ethical problem. He decided to continue along the lane, in order to overtake whoever else was upon it—for the new footprints still punctured the white way—or, failing that, to try to establish contact with the outer world.

The snow increased a little, and the transition from more or less open land to a thickly wooded lane made the going difficult. The tall trees gloomed up into the flecked darkness like giant ghosts, and as the lane did not run straight but wound through them, they seemed to be playing an ironic game with the lonely intruder by continually moving and flitting into his way. He walked right into one before he realised he had strayed from the

track. The branches brushed his forehead icily. It took him three
minutes to find the lane again, and he swore at himself for losing time. The unknown person ahead of him must have gained
a valuable advantage during those wasted minutes, and in order
to make up the deficiency David tried to increase his pace. The
result was a header, with more mouthfuls of snow.

"I am having a lovely Christmas Eve!" he reflected, as he clam-
bered to his feet. "How long do I go on before I give up?"

The gloomy house he had left behind him seemed a haven
of delight by comparison with the lonely, inclement region he
was now travelling through. The house contained creeps, but it
also contained warm fires, comfortable chairs—excluding the
dining-room chair Jessie had first sat in—and, above all, people.
Here he merely had the company of spectres. He began to wonder whether it was a spectre he was tracking.

Whether material or ethereal, his quarry refused to reveal
itself, though the marks of its journey continued like the clues
of a paper-chase.

"I suppose I'll be able to find my way back?" thought David
suddenly.

On the point of pausing to consider his position, he spied
something ahead of him at last. For a moment, in his bemused
mental condition, he actually thought it was a ghost, for it
seemed to flit out of the trees and then to flit back again as
though propelled and withdrawn by some occult agency. The
retreat had been as swift and as unexpected as the advance.

But then the form reappeared, and remained motionless.
It had turned in his direction, and it waited without moving
while he hurried forward. And when he was near enough to dis-
tinguish it as a definite human figure, new emotions began to
replace the old and to give his numb brain a fresh impetus. The

new emotions were surprise and anxiety mixed with a wholly selfish secret pleasure. The figure was that of a girl in evident distress.

Quickly his sympathy passed from himself to her.

"Hallo!" he called out, making his voice as hale and hearty as he could to counteract the uncanny atmosphere through which it echoed. "In trouble?"

"My God, yes!" came the girl's response.

The voice was cultured, and sent a little warm thrill through him.

"What is it?" he asked. "I'll help."

He had reached her by now, and had received his first glimpse of her beauty. Some may have thought Lydia more beautiful, for Lydia possessed a brilliance that could disturb the night rest of many men, but a brother is never a true judge of his own sister, and to David this girl's beauty transcended Lydia's a thousandfold, even though her features were not clear to him in the darkness. He was conscious, however, of the softness of those features, of the delicate contours, and of the long lashes that framed the anxious eyes. He was also conscious of the depth of the eyes as they shone through their anxiety with new hope.

"This way!" she gulped. "Our car's stuck. My father—I'm afraid he's ill!"

A few moments previously, David's mind had been swamped with problems. Now they all vanished in the girl's. Ghosts, screams, corpses, murderers—all became secondary matters beside the girl's distress. Not because it was more important in the scheme of things, but because of the strange power that lies in a woman to disturb a man's balance and eliminate his sense of proportion.

She turned, and led him along the lane from which she had appeared. She had not, as he had first imagined, materialised from trees, but had come out from a fork on the right. A little way along the fork, tilted into a ditch and half-submerged in snow, was a small saloon car.

"Whew!" murmured David. "When did this happen?"

"About an hour ago," answered the girl. "At least, I think so—I've lost count of time."

"And your father's inside?"

"Yes."

"Right! I'll get him out."

But to his surprise she laid a detaining hand on his sleeve.

"No, wait a moment!" she exclaimed.

"Why?"

"He's all right in there—I mean, he's gone to sleep. If we wake him and get him in the road, what will we do?"

"You mean, he's better where he is till we decide?"

"Yes. Only, of course, I want you to have a look at him."

The door was jammed. The girl had got out somehow through the window. David peered into the car, and managed to get a sufficiently close scrutiny of the elderly man in the corner to satisfy his immediate anxiety. The man was breathing quietly, and gave no outward sign of being in distress.

"He seems all right," he said reassuringly. "Did he get a knock?"

"No."

"But you said he was ill?"

"Well, he had a shock. My mind isn't working very well. I think I'm still a bit confused. And then, the weather. He can't stand much."

"You've had a shock, too."

"Yes. Both. It was madness to come out, but he insisted. I mean—on a night like this! They told us we could never do it. Once he makes up his mind, though, you can't move him. I think I'm talking too much."

"I think you need to talk," he replied, "and I certainly want to hear all you've got to say. Where are you trying to get to?"

"A house called Valley House. Do you know it?" she asked.

"I'm afraid I don't. I'm a stranger in the neighbourhood, as they say."

"So am I. I don't know it, either—I've never been there before. But it must be somewhere near here. We came by train to Hemmersby—that's the station for it—and then stopped at an inn. I thought we were going to stay there the night—we ought to have—but father suddenly got restless, and insisted on trying it. Once he makes up his mind—oh, I told you that!" She gave a sudden little self-conscious laugh. "You see the silly state I'm in. I'm not usually like this, but this whole trip has sent me all to pieces."

"We'll soon put the pieces together again."

"I think it was being here all alone for so long, and waiting, and nothing happening. I'm better already now I've met some one."

"What were you waiting for?"

"Yes, I haven't told you. Father was driving. We couldn't get any one to bring us, but they let us have the car, and father said he knew the way. We got hopelessly lost, as you can imagine, and after getting stuck I don't know how many times, we finally landed in this ditch."

"What did your father do then?"

She did not answer immediately. It sounded a simple question, but she seemed to have difficulty in finding the right reply.

"Well, I don't think he knew what to do, any more than I did," she said. "He—he's not been too well lately, and I expect the whole thing confused him."

He knew she was holding something back, and wondered how he could draw it from her.

"I suppose he got out of the car?"

"No. He just—well, that's what rather worried me. I—I don't think I can explain."

"Don't try, if it hurts."

She looked at him quickly. He loved her eyes at that moment. He found he was trying not to love her altogether. "Because that's just too ridiculous!" he told himself.

"I think I'm rather lucky," she replied. "You're understanding." Her voice became steadier, as though his understanding had eased the tension inside her. "I'll try and explain. You see, we—I've got to look after him."

" 'We' was right," David smiled.

She turned her head away for an instant. When she looked at him again there was a suspicious brightness in her eyes. "Yes, now I'm sure I'm lucky.... My father isn't—what? You see, I'm stuck at once. He isn't the same as most people. Please don't misunderstand that. I only mean he's apt to be—dreamy—absent-minded—and so sometimes I don't know whether he's ill or whether it's just that. Lately I've been more worried than ever. I wanted to go somewhere else for Christmas, but he would come here—I don't know why." She stopped, astonished at herself. "Why am I saying all this?" she exclaimed.

"I can tell you, if you'll let me," answered David.

"Go on, then."

"It's because it's been bottled up inside you too long and the cork has been just bursting to pop—and because *I'm* lucky, too, and want to hear."

"Yes, perhaps.... After the accident, he got—like I've described. Dreamy and absent-minded. Really, almost as though he *had* had a bad knock and it had stunned him. Only he hadn't. All he would say was, 'Well, it's happened—don't worry—it will all work out.' Things of that kind. Till he got drowsy—I couldn't rouse him—and went to sleep."

David turned to the car again, and once more poked his head through the window. The occupant was in the same position as before. Breathing peacefully, and to all appearances sleeping comfortably. There was a vague smile on his round, smooth face. David got an odd impression that he was a man who had not completely grown up.

"I don't think you need worry about him at the moment," he said, turning back to the girl. "I'm sure he's all right, but of course we've got to get him somewhere—and you, too. What was the name of the house you're making for?"

"Valley House," she answered.

"They expect you there?"

"Oh, yes."

"Perhaps they've sent out, and are trying to find you."

"I don't think that's likely."

"But you said something about waiting——"

"Yes, I haven't told you about that. A man came by here some while ago, and I called to him. If I hadn't, he'd have gone right by. He promised to get some help. But he didn't.... What's the matter?"

"Nothing!" replied David quickly. "When was this? How long ago?"

"I don't know," she returned. "My watch has stopped, and I've lost count."

"Ten minutes?"

"Oh, no, much longer."

"An hour?"

"It must be, nearly."

"What sort of a man was he?" As she began to look startled, he added, "I passed a man myself, and was just wondering whether it was the same one."

"A labourer, I should think," she replied. "I couldn't see him very well."

"You heard his voice, though?"

"Yes."

"And was that like a labourer's?"

"Yes. Common."

While David thought, "That was Smith!" her next remark confirmed it.

"I didn't like him very much—he was in too great a hurry. It was partly because of him that I was afraid to go far from the car—I didn't want to leave Father alone."

"You were quite right," nodded David. "It was a rotten position to be in, and so far I haven't done very much to relieve it! By the way, did you see anybody else? After Smith?" She stared at him in astonishment, and he mutely swore at himself for his slip. "That's a habit of mine," he explained lamely. "In our family we always call common people Smith. Did you see anybody after him?"

"Only you."

"That means," reflected David, "that the other person—the one I was following—didn't pass this way, but continued along the other fork of the lane."

"You don't mind if I don't believe that about Smith, do you?" came the girl's voice.

"Not in the least," he replied, "so long as it doesn't worry you. Then I *would* mind. Talking of names, could we exchange ours? Mine's David Carrington."

"Mine's Nora Strange."

"Thank you. Now, the next step, Miss Strange, is to——"

But the next step was provided with startling abruptness by Nora's father in the car. Suddenly opening his eyes, he called out:

"Who are you talking to, Nora? Is that Shaw?"

David's head swam as he recalled that Shaw was the name of the vanished servant!

CHAPTER XIX

ADDITIONS TO THE PARTY

FOR a moment or two David could merely stand and stare. He had passed from situation to situation, struggling to master each new development without deserting the last, but now a development had occurred that was beyond his logic to understand or his capacity to deal with. The world seemed to have turned topsy-turvy, and it would hardly have surprised him if the snowflakes themselves had started going upwards.

The man in the car had pronounced the name Shaw. That meant that the destination of these two stranded people—Valley House—was the house from which David had come; that it was for them the fires had been lit, the bedrooms prepared, and the stores laid in; and that Shaw's two afternoon visitors had not been his master and his master's daughter, whose arrival had been delayed by the weather, but two entirely different individuals. It meant that Mr. Maltby's reconstruction fell to the ground.

It meant something else, as well—something of more immediate moment. In assisting Mr. Strange and Nora to their destination, he would be taking them to a house in which he and five others were trespassing. How, leaving all other considerations aside, would they receive that news? And how, all in a moment, could he explain it to them?

"Mr. Carrington!" It was Nora's voice again. She had been watching him closely, though it needed no close scrutiny to discover his bewildered condition. "Something's the matter!"

"Yes—something is," he stammered.

"Who *is* it, Nora?" called Mr. Strange again. "Not Shaw, eh? Who is it?"

"Just some one who's going to help us, father," the girl called back. "Don't worry, dear. Stay where you are for a moment." Then she turned to David again, and lowering her voice, asked, "What?"

"I've just come from Valley House," he replied, deciding that simple truth was the only possible solution, "though I didn't know that was the name of the house till now."

"How do you know it now?"

"Shaw—the name of the servant."

"I see. Of course, he's there."

"No, he's not."

"But he must be! Or do you mean he's out, looking for us?"

"Not even that. The house was empty when we arrived——"

"We?"

"I and several others. Our train got stuck in a snowdrift, we tried to cut across to Hemmersby, lost ourselves—as you have done—and eventually staggered into your house for shelter."

"Do you mean they're there now?" she exclaimed.

"They can't get away," he answered.

"But you were trying to?"

"Something of the sort. I expect you think our behaviour quite unforgivable——"

"Oh, no!" she interrupted. "Of course not! Do you think to-night I'd hesitate to find any shelter I could for myself and my father, whose ever house it was? But I don't understand why the house was empty! Shaw should have been there."

"He wasn't."

She thought for a moment, glanced back at the car—her father was reclining in his corner again, waiting with almost uncanny patience—and then said:

"There's something else I don't understand, Mr. Carrington. If our servant wasn't there, and if you haven't seen him, how did you know his name was Shaw?"

"Miss Strange," replied David, "you are not only a very nice person, you are a very intelligent person, and that was a very intelligent question. Will you go on being intelligent, please, and let all these matters wait till I get you into your house? That's the first job, isn't it? Your coat is simply soaking, and your father needs a fire as much as you do. I may say we've had the cheek to keep the home fires blazing, and as one of the intruders you'll find there is my sister who is just aching to make some return for what we've received, you can be certain she'll give you any help either you or your father want. So will you trust me till then—and can we make a start?"

"Of course I trust you," she answered at once, "and you're quite right. You know the way?"

"I hope so. Anyhow, we'll have a shot at it."

With difficulties looming ahead, it was an immense relief to find that Mr. Strange himself presented none. In fact, his attitude was unnaturally obedient, and after Nora had whispered a few words to him through the window—David stood tactfully aside while the whispered conversation was going on—he allowed himself to be helped out of the car and became a perfectly passive member of the party.

"I suppose he *hasn't* had a knock?" David wondered.

He showed no signs of damage, and Nora had limited the physical results of the accident to shock, but he did not seem at this moment like a stubborn man who could make up his mind and then refuse to alter it. David was not surprised that Nora was worried over her father's condition, and guessed that there might be even more cause than she had so far admitted.

"This is very good of you," were Mr. Strange's first words to David, when he stood in the road and turned up his coat collar. "I knew some one would come along."

"Well, I'm an optimist, too, sir," answered David. "I've even told your daughter that I'm going to find the way back to your house."

"Back? Oh, of course—she mentioned something about——"

His voice trailed off, and David and Nora glanced at each other. Nora's expression implied, "You see what I mean."

"Feeling all right for the journey?" inquired David.

"Quite all right for the journey," replied Mr. Strange. "Nothing can interfere with the journey. Not even, as you will note, a car accident." He turned to his daughter with a faint smile. "I was right at the inn—I said we would get there."

"We haven't quite got there yet, Father," returned Nora.

"No, but we shall. It is fortunate we left most of our luggage at the station and only have our light bags. As a matter of fact, Mr. Carrington—that is the name?—there was no alternative, because in the confusion at the station the luggage got left behind. Once we blamed the war for everything. I recall that well. I went through the war. To-night, we blame the snow. Though personally, in regard to the luggage, I am inclined to think ... However."

"Let's start," exclaimed Nora nervily.

"Yes, come along," answered David. "And I'm going to suggest that we link arms. It's easy to get lost."

"A good idea," nodded Mr. Strange. "Over the top into No Man's Land, eh? Is it far?"

Anxious to get as many points clear as he could before returning to further complications, David tackled one that had been bothering him.

"Valley House is your place, sir, isn't it?" he asked.

"It is certainly my place," agreed Mr. Strange. "No one can take it away from me."

"Then *you* ought to be leading the way, not me," commented David.

"In daylight, I might do so," answered Mr. Strange, "although it is a long while—many years—since I was there, but to-night I got lost, and frankly I have no idea where we are. How long, do you suppose, it will take us to walk?"

"Well—continuing to be an optimist—I should say about twenty minutes to half an hour. Probably nearer half an hour. But my time's got mixed up, Miss Strange, like yours. That's just a wild guess."

"I hope it's a good one," she replied, "or we won't be there before Christmas."

"Christmas," repeated Mr. Strange thoughtfully. "Yes— Christmas."

They had begun to walk, and David felt Nora's arm tighten slightly against his.

Reaching the spot where the lanes had forked, David gave a quick glance along the fork he had not taken and noticed that the footprints he had been following, by now almost filled in, continued in that direction. This confirmed what he had gathered from Nora's information—that Smith had taken the right fork while the other person had taken the left. Who that other person was, and why he—or she—had not been accompanied by his—or her—companion, he now had not the slightest notion.

They were now in the narrow lane which he himself had come along, and the game of turning and twisting began again. Conversation was postponed by mutual consent as, with heads lowered, they grappled with the grim task of beating the blizzard. In spite of his optimism, which was alleged rather than actual, David made a poor guide, and on three separate occasions they blundered off their route to find themselves in a white maze of towering trees and tangled foliage. On the third occasion, while they groped around for over ten minutes in the freezing forest silence, David found himself nearly giving up hope, and he became acutely conscious that Nora was also fighting panic. Mr. Strange, on the other hand, accepted the situation with an almost irritating calmness, either buoyed up by some secret philosophy he refused to share, or immune from emotion through numbness. Or perhaps his condition was due to a combination of both causes. He walked stiffly, and his frozen feet frequently stumbled

Rediscovering the lane at last, they met once more the full flurry of the falling flakes, while a below-zero breeze rose out of nowhere and played dismal music on their backs. Suddenly Nora felt a swift tug on her arm, and almost fell against her guide as he pulled her away from the side of the lane towards the middle.

"What was that?" she gasped.

"Sorry," murmured David in reply. "I just thought you might trip over that mound.... We're nearly there."

He had recognised a landmark.

They emerged from the wooded lane into the open. The snow was working up to its full fury again, and David had a queer sensation that the storm had been temporarily decreased by Fate so that this particular part of its programme could be played. He could never have undertaken this journey—nor could others have undertaken theirs—if the snowstorm had consistently maintained its present height.

"Much farther?" asked the girl, through half-closed teeth.

"No," he answered, straining his snow-clogged eyes. "We'll probably see the lights in a minute. Hang on to me."

A light developed as he spoke. Like the headlights of a bus in a thick London fog, it did not reveal itself until they were almost up to it. It was the light in the back passage, shining through the still-open window.

"Home!" murmured David, almost sick with relief.

CHAPTER XX
THE NEW ARRIVALS

DURING that tortuous journey Mr. Strange had shown the fewest outward signs of distress, but when he had been helped up the slope of snow beneath the back window, and then pushed and pulled into the passage, he peacefully collapsed. Mr. Maltby, Mr. Hopkins and Lydia had been on the spot to assist his ingress, and when his surprising appearance was followed by the appearance of Nora and David, looking not far off collapse themselves, there had ensued a moment of complete bewilderment. It was during this moment that Mr. Strange closed his eyes and slid quietly to the floor.

"Another patient, and this time our host," announced David.

"What's that?" exclaimed Mr. Maltby.

"Mr. Strange and his daughter—just arrived." David added the last two words significantly, for Mr. Maltby's benefit, and their meaning was not lost upon him. "We must get them to their rooms. Explanations later."

Then a rather surprising thing happened. As David moved to the recumbent form, Mr. Hopkins sprang forward and pushed him back.

"No, no, you've done enough!" he cried. "Let me!"

A genuine spirit of service had at last entered into him, and he bent down and began struggling more zealously than skilfully with Mr. Strange's legs.

"Thanks—but I think it needs two of us," said David. "And perhaps you'll look after Miss Strange, Lydia? She's been through a pretty stiff time."

But Lydia did not need the hint. She already had her arm round Nora, and was beginning the good offices her brother had predicted.

Christmas crept in almost unnoticed. Only Jessie Noyes, ruminating on the couch by the hall fire, was conscious of the chiming of midnight. All the others, with the exception of Thomson who was still asleep, in the drawing-room, were engaged in various occupations upstairs, too absorbed to attend to the advent of the twenty-fifth. "I said, 'A merry Christmas,'" ran Jessie's diary, "but there was no one to hear me, unless you count that portrait on the wall. He seemed to hear me, in fact, he seemed to hear everything, but he didn't wish me a merry Christmas back, thank God. But after all I'd been through it wouldn't have surprised me much if he had, though I expect if he really had I'd have gone off pop!"

Mr. Hopkins was the first to descend to the hall, which by virtue of its comfort and spaciousness, its lavish furnishing, and its large brick fireplace, had become the common centre. Jessie glanced at him rather apprehensively, for this was the first time they had been alone together since he had entered her bedroom; but he seemed in a chastened spirit. Recent events and emotions had had their effect upon him, and given him the team attitude.

"Well, that's done!" he exclaimed, a little over-loudly. Ghosts don't like loud voices, which was why he did. "We've got Mr. Strange upstairs—bit of a weight, between you and me—and now he's sound between sheets."

"Which sheets?" asked Jessie.

"Eh? Well, as a matter of fact, he's in the room *you* had. Personally I—er—wasn't quite sure whether that was the best place to put him, but—well, there you are."

"I hope he'll be all right."

"I expect so. Maltby said that it was only because—that is——"

His voice trailed off. About to sit on the end of her couch, he changed his mind and sank down into an arm-chair.

"Because of what?" she inquired.

"Well, I don't suppose you want to speak about it."

"You mean—what I felt?"

"Yes. Must have been damned nasty."

"It was!"

"Not only the bed, you know, but that chair in the dining-room, too. Extraordinary case. Yes, and I've *come* across some extraordinary cases in my time. Not sure that this doesn't beat the lot. What do *you* make of it all?"

Mr. Hopkins evidently did want to speak about it. The fact was, he badly needed conversation with somebody who did not develop his inferiority complex, and although he had made a bad start with Jessie, he still felt that she was the only person in the house who could speak his language.

"I don't know what to make of it," answered Jessie.

"Of course, the hammer just capped it," he exclaimed. "I've come across a similar case, though. South America. They touched an old woman's forehead with a piece of wood—it was a bit of an aeroplane that had crashed—did I tell you? —no, you weren't here—and she—what's the matter?"

"I don't know what you're talking about!" said Jessie, staring at him.

"Eh?"

"What hammer?"

Mr. Hopkins grew suddenly pink.

"Oh, well, never mind," he murmured. "Forget that."

"No, please tell me!"

"All right, I suppose I must now—and, after all, why not? Only I wouldn't let 'em know I'm telling you—mind you, I think you ought to know—but they'll say I've put my foot in it. All this damned secretiveness—well, let it go. It was when you were in that trance——"

"Trance?"

"I mean, sleep. When you were asleep. You talked in your sleep—yes, that's it. And you said the hammer had hit you. Well, we knew it had hit some one, so that didn't really get us much farther.... . Of course, I know what *I* think. However, what's the good of talking, when everybody else knows better?" He shrugged his shoulders. "Queer business. But don't worry. If there's any trouble, I'll look after you."

He glanced at her to see how she took the suggestion. Her grave expression puzzled and worried him.

"Do you know what I'm thinking?" she said. "I'm thinking it's best when I look after myself."

"Well, that's all right, if you can."

"I expect I can. I always have." Suddenly she added, "Anyhow, Mr. Hopkins, I don't want *you* to!"

"I see you've not forgiven me," he frowned.

Something in his expression made her feel a beast, as she admitted later in her diary.

"If there's anything to forgive, of course I forgive you!" she exclaimed. "Don't think anything more about it."

He brightened.

A few moments later Mr. Maltby and David joined them. That, Mr. Hopkins thought, was a pity, but he dared not show his displeasure lest he should again fall from grace. His one hope of maintaining friendly relations with Jessie was to continue the team spirit and to prove that she had misjudged him.

"Well, how's things?" he asked. "All O.K.?"

"That is rather overestimating the beauty of the situation," replied Mr. Maltby.

"Ah!" said Mr. Hopkins. He hoped Jessie was noting how well he was taking the old man's acidity. "But no fresh trouble, eh?"

"Considerable, in my estimation. But Mr. Strange is asleep— that, at least is satisfactory—and Miss Strange will be coming down shortly."

"Coming down? What for?" exclaimed Mr. Hopkins. "I should have thought she'd have got straight to bed!"

"No one can think of bed to-night unless their condition forces it."

"She's coming down to tell her story," explained David. "She's got one."

"I see," murmured Mr. Hopkins. "She didn't tell it to you, then?"

"Only odd scraps," replied David.

"And, so far, I have only had odd scraps of your own story," said Mr. Maltby "This would be a good moment to tell it in detail."

"Yes, sir, I agree. But—here, or in the dining room?"

Jessie caught the glance he gave in her direction.

"Here," she decided for them. "When will you all learn that there's nothing so frightening as to be left in the dark? And, any-how, I know more than you think I do already—I know about that hammer!" Mr. Hopkins began to look flustered, but she quickly came to his rescue. "I made Mr. Hopkins tell me. I had to drag it out of him."

"Damn good little sport!" thought Mr. Hopkins, as he let the white lie pass. "I'll do something for her one of these days, see if I don't!"

"In that case, let it be here," said Mr. Maltby, "and please don't omit any point, however trivial it may seem. A thread of cotton has hung a man before now. When you left us——" He glanced at the clock. "Oh, a merry Christmas, everybody. When you left us an hour and forty-three minutes ago, and went out through the back window...?"

David told his story. Obedient to Mr. Maltby's request, he described his journey as minutely as he could, giving his reasons as well as his facts. He dwelt particularly on the various foot-prints he had seen and followed, giving their character, condi-tion, and direction. The one part of the story he hurried over was that relating to the mound of snow. He was relieved that Mr. Maltby did not press on this point.

When he had finished, the old man took one or two turns up and down the carpet, and then asked:

"Will you please repeat all you have told me about those footprints? I want to get them quite fixed in my mind."

David did so.

"Thank you. And your theory was that the fainter footprints were made by Smith, and that the fresher and more distinct ones were made by somebody else, probably one of the two people I saw hurrying away before I arrived here?"

"Yes, and who we now know were *not* Mr. and Miss Strange."

"Exactly. And Smith went by the Stranges' stranded car?"

"That seems fairly certain."

"Fairly certain is not quite certain, but for the moment we will accept that. And the other person, who was not Mr. or Miss

Strange, did *not* go by the stranded car, but took the left road where the lane forked?"

"You've got it exactly."

"Yes, exactly. I've got it exactly that this person did not know a car was stranded, or that Mr. and Miss Strange were in it, or that Mr. and Miss Strange are here at all. That may not be in the least important. On the other hand, it may be very important indeed." He paused, then went on, "What I have not got so exactly is why this person who was neither Mr. nor Miss Strange, but who is alleged to have been one of the two people I saw hurrying away—and who might still, remember, have been the servant Charles Shaw—and who might *not*—should have remained in this neighbourhood for over six hours. After having—we assume—dropped a certain hammer."

"He——"

"Or she," interposed Mr. Maltby. "Avoid the fixed idea."

"He or she may have been looking for the hammer."

"Or for something else."

"I thought of that, too."

"And may still be looking for it."

"He—or she—has gone too far away now."

"You went some distance yourself, but you came back. If this unknown person stayed around here for over six hours because through wanting something very badly, and if he or she has not got that something, there may be more footprints in the snow before long. In this direction. I do not quarrel with anything you did on your journey, Mr. Carrington, but I wish it could have happened that you had traced those first fresh footsteps—the ones round the house—backwards a little farther. I should like to know where they started from."

"Shall I have a shot to find out now?" asked David.

"Goodness, haven't you done enough?" murmured Jessie.

"What about me?" suggested Mr. Hopkins, praying the offer would be vetoed. "Shall *I* go?"

Mr. Maltby shook his head, and turned towards the staircase.

"I think we will leave that for the moment," he said. "Here comes Miss Strange, and the next thing we need is *her* story."

CHAPTER XXI

NORA'S STORY

THERE was a general movement as Nora Strange came down the stairs, and David jumped quickly to his feet. Without her heavy coat—she was wearing a white silk blouse and light brown skirt—some ethereal quality in her seemed to be accentuated, but it was not the ghostly quality that lay around Valley House like a dank mist. It was something delicately fragile, that gave her a human luminosity.

"Feeling better?" asked David.

"Much," she answered. "Thanks to your sister."

"Lydia knows all the right things to do," he said. "Where is she?"

"She's sitting in father's room. She's going to let us know when he needs anything."

"Good. Well, come and sit down and get warm."

"Yes, sit here," added Jessie, moving her legs to make room on the couch. "This is the best place, I mustn't hog it."

"Thank you."

"And what about food?" asked David, as Nora settled herself against a corner. "Can we get you something?"

"No, I'm not hungry. We had a big meal at the inn before we left."

The two other men were regarding her silently. Her type of beauty, as Lydia's, was beyond the reach of such sensualists as Mr. Hopkins, and although he would have awarded both Lydia and Nora higher marks than Jessie in a Beauty Contest, he infinitely preferred the chorus girl's prettiness because his experience had proved it more accessible. Mr. Maltby's interest in Nora

Strange, on the other hand, was purely academic. Now he suddenly addressed her, and said:

"In that case, Miss Strange, may we talk?"

"Yes, of course," she answered. "That's what I've come down for."

"Then let us first get the obvious courtesies out of the way, because we have more important things to talk about," replied Mr. Maltby. "Are you forgiving us for our intrusion?"

"Oh, yes!"

"As a matter of fact, it may turn out, from your point of view, a fortunate intrusion. If we had not been here, Mr. Carrington would not have found you in the lane, and even if you had succeeded without him in bringing your father here——"

"I never should!"

"That we do not know. But you would have been in a very difficult position if you had arrived here alone, and had had to find out certain things which now I shall be able to tell you. You see, Miss Strange, we have a story, too, to exchange for yours, and I have no doubt that many of the details will dovetail. If you and your father need any help, we are here to give it to you."

"You've helped us already."

"We shall go on doing so. Please bear that in mind when you are telling us whatever you care to tell us of the circumstances of this visit. This is, naturally, not idle curiosity. Mr. Carrington tells me that this is your first visit to this house?"

"Yes."

"But it belongs to your father?"

"Yes. It was left to him by *his* father." She glanced at the picture over the mantelpiece. "It had to be—it's what is called entailed property."

"I see. And that is a picture of your grandfather?"

"I think it must be."

"You never saw him yourself, then?"

"No. I was only a baby when—when he died. But——"

"One moment. Did he die here? In this house?"

"Yes."

"That would be about twenty years ago?"

"How did you know?"

"You said you were a baby at the time," smiled Mr. Maltby. "I put your age at about twenty, and then did a very simple sum. Forgive the interruption. I shall probably interrupt you a lot. Has anybody told you my name? It is Edward Maltby. If you are interested in psychic matters and read occult literature you may have heard of it, but otherwise you will not. You were telling me how you recognised that picture of your grandfather whom you never saw?"

"I recognise it because it looks something like my father," she answered, rather breathlessly. David gathered that, in her tired condition, she was finding it rather difficult to keep pace with Mr. Maltby's quick mind. Mr. Maltby never seemed to tire. "And then I once saw an old photograph of him. My grandfather."

"Only one?"

"Yes."

"Your father does not keep an extensive family album, then?"

"What's he asking that for?" wondered David.

But he knew that every question put by the old man had a reason.

"No, we haven't one. I don't think my father——" She paused suddenly. "No, that doesn't come into the story."

"You are utterly wrong," retorted Mr. Maltby. "It does come into the story. Everything you can tell me about your grandfather comes into the story. And if you only tell me half the story, I shall not be able to help you. Your grandfather—his death—your father—his reason for coming here—your servant or caretaker, Charles Shaw—any other people or near relatives who have lived in this house or had anything to do with it—I want the whole lot. My mouth is wide open, Miss Strange, for anything you can tell me. You find me in the greediest possible mood!"

"May I make an interruption?" interposed David.

"That, Miss Strange, is how Mr. Carrington generally begins his interruptions," remarked Mr. Maltby, "but he interrupts whether he receives permission or not."

"Then I won't make this any exception," answered David, "although *you* may think this interruption a rude one, Mr. Maltby."

"That does not worry me. I can be rude myself."

"Queen Anne's dead," murmured Mr. Hopkins, getting in a quiet hit.

David turned to Nora, who was looking a little helpless.

"What I want to say is this, Miss Strange. Mr. Maltby—yes, that man who is watching me at this moment to see how rude I am going to be—is a dry old fossil with a manner that sometimes reminds one of the dissecting-room. But even when he is rudest he has a heart of gold—that is the sugar on the pill, sir—and he gets there. So this is my advice. Don't be bullied in your own house——"

"Her father's," corrected the subject of the discourse.

"—or be put off by his interruptions, for which *he* never asks permission. Don't tell us a thing you don't want to. But tell us all you can!"

Nora smiled. She knew that he was trying, for her sake, to remove the atmosphere of the dissecting-room, and she was grateful.

"I haven't felt that anybody has been rude," she answered, "and I will tell you all I can. I'm not quite sure where to begin, though."

"There is a gentleman up on the wall," replied Mr. Maltby, "who, I think, is asking you to begin with his death."

"No, I must begin a little before that—if I'm really going to tell you everything," she said. "My grandfather was living here with my father and my uncle. My father wasn't married then. I believe there were ructions sometimes—my father and uncle didn't get on very well together, and father told me he was quite glad to leave the place when the war broke out. He joined up at once."

"That was twenty-three years ago."

"Yes."

"Did your uncle join up, too?"

"No. I think there was something the matter with him, but I'm not sure. Anyhow, he didn't. He stayed on here. My father says he said they only needed very young men, but my father was two years older than Uncle Harvey, and *he* went."

"How old was your father?"

"He's fifty-seven now. He must have been thirty-four."

"The age limit was raised well above that. Probably your Uncle Harvey did have something the matter with him—or found a way of getting excused. There were plenty of ways—and plenty of people to look for them. Would you say your Uncle Harvey was that kind of man? Or am I getting too personal?" he added, with a dry glance at David.

"Not at all. I should think he *was* that kind of man. I needn't hide from you that father doesn't like him—and he doesn't like father."

"Could it be put more strongly?"

"I dare say."

"In fact, not to mince matters, they hate each other?"

"Yes, but from a distance—they haven't seen each other for years. After the war had been on about two years, my father met my mother—she was an actress, and he was on leave—and on his next leave—it was at Christmas—he proposed to her and brought her here. There was a bad scene. I think—I think my grandfather must have been rather a peculiar person. He had to have his own way, and father thinks he was jealous, too. That may have had something to do with it."

"But your father wasn't a boy!" exclaimed Mr. Maltby. "By that time he was thirty-six!"

"I know. It was ridiculous. Anyway, grandfather wouldn't give his approval, and threatened to cut father out of his will if he went on with it."

"But, of course, your father did go on with it?"

"Of course. He could be stubborn, too. So grandfather turned them out of the house, and altered his will in my uncle's favour. Then——"

"Wait a moment," interrupted Mr. Maltby. "There are one or two points I want to get straight. Christmas. Rather interesting, that. It would be the Christmas of 1916, eh? Exactly twenty-one years ago?"

"Yes."

"Rather a coincidence that it's Christmas again, while you're sitting here, telling us about it? Or not? Probably not. Of course, if this house is entailed property, your grandfather couldn't cut your father out of that."

"No, but he cut him out of everything else."

"Everything?"

"Absolutely."

"Yes, your grandfather must have been a very peculiar man. But then, many excellent people are peculiar. I am myself. And vain, too. I refer now to your grandfather again, for vanity is not one of my faults. That hair—glance at it! A man of over sixty, with smooth dark hair like that! He must have taken extraordinary care of it. You may recall, Mr. Carrington, that hair was one of the first things I noticed in the picture.... Remarkable.... Tell me, Miss Strange, had your grandfather a grudge against your father? By refusing his approval and cutting him out of his will, do you suppose he was paying off an old score—or expressing some prejudice, eh?"

"Oh, no!" exclaimed Nora. "That was the funny part of it. He always preferred my father to Uncle Harvey."

"I see. Well, human nature is odd, and often works like that. Your Uncle Harvey, I expect, was quite pleased?"

"I don't know. Very likely."

"Extremely likely. Well, continue. No, something else. Charles Shaw. The servant. Was he a member of the staff at that time?"

"Yes. He's been with the family for over forty years—that's why father keeps him on——"

"As servant when he is here, and as caretaker when he is not here. And generally he is not here. In your grandfather's day I suppose Shaw was the butler?"

"I think so."

"Thank you. Well, your father married your mother, and was cut out of the will for doing what any right-minded man would have done in his place. I have never married, but if I wanted to, nothing should stop me. Yes, and then?"

"Then," continued Nora, who by this time was acclimatising herself to the old man's methods, "my father returned to the front. I was born while he was away."

"In 1917."

"Yes. I think my mother wrote to my grandfather, but I've never been sure of that, and I don't think father knows, either. It must have been a confusing year for them. Not only because of my coming—and the war—but father got shell-shock. And my grandfather fell ill, too.... . Shell-shock can last a long time, you know. I mean, the effects of it."

"Your father has never quite got over the effects of it, Miss Strange, has he?" asked David.

"I don't think so," she answered. "He—his health has never been really good ever since I can remember him."

"You told me he was apt to be dreamy and absent-minded."

"Yes. I think the shell-shock has had something to do with it. He gets—fixed ideas, and thinks about them."

"Would you mention any of his fixed ideas?" inquired Mr. Maltby.

"Well, one is that there is going to be another war."

"That fixed idea is not born only of shell-shock."

"No, of course not. Another has been about this house. He's always been convinced that he'd come back here—but I'll come to that in a few moments. I want to tell you now about what you were first asking me—grandfather's death. He fell ill, as I told you. It was about the same time that father came back with shell-shock. But on Christmas Eve father—he was better then—received a sudden invitation for him and my mother to come to Valley House at once. It astonished them. They didn't understand it. But grandfather said he had a surprise for them, and that they weren't to refer to it until he told them what it was himself." She stopped, and gave a little involuntary shiver. "But they never heard what it was. Grandfather died—just before he could tell it to them."

She dried up suddenly. No one spoke for a few seconds. Then Mr. Maltby said quietly:

"He may tell it yet."

"What do you mean?" exclaimed Nora.

"Probably nothing," answered the old man.

"How long had your grandfather been ill?"

"I don't know exactly. Several months."

"Two? Three? Six?"

"I believe about three."

"When is your birthday?"

"October."

"The what?"

"The third."

"And when did your father return to England with shell-shock?"

"I think it was a week or two after I was born."

"And he did not go to Valley House between then and Christmas Day? That is, between his arrival in England in the first half of October, 1917, and December 25th, 1917?"

"No."

"What was the matter with your grandfather?"

"It was his heart."

"And that's what he died of? Heart trouble?"

"Yes. He was in bed when my father and mother arrived——"

"But he did not die in his bed!"

"How do you know?"

"I can take you to the chair he died in." She stared at him in amazement, while Jessie shuddered. "It is in the dining-room now. Was it in the dining-room then?"

"I suppose—no, it couldn't have been—it must have been brought in here for him, then——"

"Here! The hall!"

Mr. Maltby jumped up from the stool on which he had been squatting.

"Yes! Quite so! He's come down from his bedroom. The four-poster bed. Pale—very pale. But he's come down. Dogged does it! He's down—here he is—moving to the chair—yes, but you're just as pale, Shaw, aren't you? The flesh worried you as much as the picture—only not for quite so long——"

He sat down again.

"Shaw was here?" he asked. "In the hall?"

"Yes!" gasped Nora, her eyes wide.

"Don't worry—he gets like that!" muttered Mr. Hopkins.

"And who else?" went on Mr. Maltby. "Who else were here?"

"My father and mother—Uncle Harvey—the nurse, and the doctor."

"He had a nurse, eh?"

"Yes."

"What was her name?"

"Martha—that's all father told me."

"Martha! Yes, and the doctor's?"

"Dr. Wick."

"Wick! Wick! And all these were present when he died, eh?"

"Yes. And they'd tried hard not to let him come down. You see, father and mother didn't arrive till very late—they'd had a long journey, and it was about midnight when they got here. Uncle Harvey didn't want to admit them, and they almost had to force their way in. Even then, they weren't allowed up, and they had to wait till grandfather came down. Father has described it all to me.... It seems so strange that it all happened here—where we're sitting. Grandfather called for champagne, took a sip, and then said, 'A happy Christmas to everybody, and a toast to——' That was all. He dropped the glass, fell back in his chair, and was dead the next moment."

"Heart failure," murmured Mr. Maltby, as she finished.

Nora nodded.

"And the doctor signed the certificate?"

"Yes."

"H'm. I see.... Two memorable Christmases. 1916–1917. And this is a third."

All at once he wheeled round, and shot another question.

"What time did your grandfather come down that staircase? Do you know?" he asked.

"Yes—father did mention that," replied Nora. "The clock had just struck two when grandfather finished speaking."

Then everybody saving Mr. Maltby started. The same clock struck one. Mr. Maltby turned to the portrait over the fireplace.

"In another hour," he mused, "it will be twenty years to the second since you closed your lips. Can we reopen them?"

CHAPTER XXII
LIGHTS OUT

MR. MALTBY walked to the window and drew the curtain aside. He stood looking out for several seconds, then said without turning:

"Almost stopped."

"Thank God for small mercies," muttered Mr. Hopkins.

"The mercy hasn't arrived yet," answered Mr. Maltby, "and when it does, if it does, we will have an opportunity of judging its dimensions."

"Must you always speak in riddles?" exclaimed Mr. Hopkins, as something snapped inside him. "Of course, we all know you're running this show——"

"I am not running this show," interrupted Mr. Maltby. "I did not decide the time or the date, or the moment when the snow should stop. Something infinitely bigger than myself is running the show." Then he addressed Nora. "You have not quite finished your story, Miss Strange. I would like the rest as quickly as you can tell it. Am I right in thinking your mother is no longer alive?"

"She died four years after my grandfather," answered Nora.

"In 1921, when you were four years old?"

"Yes."

"Where did you all live? Not here in this house? You mentioned that you had never been here before, though, of course, you would hardly remember it before you were four years old."

He was asking his questions through the back of his head, for his eyes were still staring out of the window.

"They put me with a nurse in London, and my mother toured in the provinces. My father was generally with her. You see, they had no money, apart from what she made."

"Who got your grandfather's money?"

"My Uncle Harvey."

"Where did he live?"

"He lived here for some time. He was supposed to pay a small rent, but he got behind-hand, and I don't think in the end he paid anything at all. Father's no good at business."

"Clearly. Shaw stayed on here with your uncle?"

"Yes, and when my uncle had run through all his money and left, Shaw still stayed to look after the place. I think it was let once or twice——"

"But Shaw saw to it that it was not let more often, eh? He was too comfortable here, with a soft job. Who paid him his wages?"

"I don't believe anybody did after Uncle Harvey went. There was a sort of arrangement that he lived rent free in return for looking after the house."

"And he possibly had a little money of his own—or some source from where to draw it," commented Mr. Maltby. "I think I've got Mr. Charles Shaw tabbed pretty accurately. Where is your uncle now?"

"We don't know."

"Did your father ever think of coming here to live himself?"

"He couldn't bear the idea. And then—you won't understand this—I don't—but he's always had a feeling that he would be called back some day, and that he had to wait till the call came. That was the other fixed idea I was telling you about."

"I see.... Yes, I see. And, this year—twenty years after—he got the call?"

"He must have."

"Don't you know in what form it came?"

"I think it was a letter. Father always avoided talking about this house and about all that happened here, and I should never have known all I do know if he hadn't got ill about two years ago. Then he told me—but when he was better he said I was to forget it. Of course, I didn't."

"What makes you think it was a letter that has brought him here now?" asked Mr. Maltby.

"Because he received one—marked 'strictly private'—three or four days ago that seemed to excite him," she replied, "but he wouldn't say what was in it. It was just after getting it that he decided to come here, and he wrote to Shaw to get everything ready."

"Where was he when he received the letter?"

"In Newcastle. He had a small class there—after mother died he made a little money—never much—by writing and teaching. He told me before we left Newcastle that he would be giving up his class.... And, ever since, he's been in this strange mood.... And that's all," she concluded.

"Yes, and the snow has stopped," said Mr. Maltby. "Mr. Carrington, did we close that back window?"

"We did," answered David.

"Well, please go and open it," said Mr. Maltby, "while I put out the light."

"Put out the light? What for?" demanded Mr. Hopkins.

Mr. Maltby did not reply, and while David made his way through the deserted kitchen to obey his instruction, the old man threw the hall into darkness, saving for the glow from the fire.

Then he went into the dining-room and extinguished the light there. Returning, he crossed to the drawing-room, peered in, and closed the door again.

"Well?" he asked, as David came back.

"I've opened it," answered David.

"What is it like outside? Can one still get in through the window?"

"Yes."

"Look here, what *is* the idea?" exclaimed Mr. Hopkins, the darkness making his voice sound twice as loud as it actually was. "Suppose some one *does* get in?"

"There are moments, Mr. Hopkins," returned Mr. Maltby, "when I refuse to believe that you are as unintelligent as you seem." To David he went on, "I think the only light upstairs is in Mr. Strange's room? Would you mind seeing to it? You can give the fire a poke, so that your sister will have some light to see by."

David departed again. Mr. Maltby drew near the fireplace, and when his figure was silhouetted against the glow he had a queer elfin aspect.

No one spoke till David returned. Jessie just managed to suppress a little shriek as a log shifted and sent out a new tongue of flame. Nora, newer to the atmosphere of Valley House and the old man's disconcerting methods, fought a sense of unreality, and sat very still. She wondered whether all these things were really happening; and, if they were, whether they emanated from an old man's wisdom or his whim.

"All lights out," announced David.

"Good!" answered Mr. Maltby. "Then we must have gone away, or else we are in bed. That's obvious, isn't it? Let us hope so. Now, then, listen! Does anybody hear anything?"

All ears were strained. Outside was utter silence. Inside, the only sound came from the ticking of the clock.

"But a few moments ago," said Mr. Maltby, "I heard Mr. Carrington open the back window, and I heard him open and close the two doors in between."

"I didn't," murmured Mr. Hopkins.

"Possibly no one did but myself. I was the only person listening for the sounds. Now, however, we will all be listening for sounds. We will be listening, not for the opening of the window, but for some one entering through the window, and dropping on to the ground with a little thud, and afterwards opening the two doors in between. In this perfect stillness we shall not miss those sounds—though I think Mr. Carrington, you might take your station by the kitchen door, to give us the first warning. Go there now, and tell me whether you can hear my voice. I am keeping it low, as now we all must." David continued his unquestioning obedience to orders, and moved to the door. "Well?"

"Quite distinct, sir," reported David, although Mr. Maltby had dropped his voice almost to a whisper.

"Then everything is set for what we may perhaps call the first scene of the last act—if, of course, there is any performance at all. Let me know if you hear anything before we do, Mr. Carrington. The moment any sound occurs, Mr. Hopkins and I will join you."

"You mean—to catch whoever it is?" inquired Mr. Hopkins sepulchrally.

"My struggling faith in your intelligence remains alive," replied Mr. Maltby. "Your voice, as well as your logic, is now satisfactory.... Miss Strange, we will continue our conversation, but although what I am about to tell you deserves full attention I am afraid it can only receive half—the other half must be reserved for that sound."

His hand moved into a side pocket, and remained there.

"Wonder if he's got a revolver?" thought Mr. Hopkins. "That old fool might have anything!" Then into his uneasy mind came another thought that could not have occurred to any one else in the room. "Wonder if he's a lunatic? God bless my soul!" But he had the sense to dismiss the theory almost as soon as it had dawned. Mr. Maltby was patently eccentric, but equally patently he was not mad.

"You have told us of two letters," said Mr. Maltby. "One—the letter from your father to Shaw advising him of your coming—I have seen. Seen sufficiently, that is, to know its contents. The other—the letter to your father supplying the incentive of this visit—I hope to see. But there is a third letter of which you know nothing—and of which nobody here knows anything but myself. I myself did not know anything about it till just after your arrival."

"Where did you find it?" inquired David.

"In Shaw's room. I went there after leaving you and your sister with Mr. Strange—you may remember, I met you again at the top of the stairs just as you were coming down yourself. The letter was on the bedroom floor." He smiled as David was about to interrupt him again. "You are about to ask, 'If it was on the floor, why didn't you find it before, when you found the letter in the waste-paper basket?' The answer is that, at that time, it was not on the floor. I have to thank Mr. Thomson for this. Even his temporary delirium—he seems to be improving now, by the way, like the weather—appears to have been especially planned.... I wonder where Smith comes into the picture?... The room was in rather a state when Thomson left it to begin his wanderings. Bedclothes all over the place, and a small table knocked over. There was a drawer in the table, and the fall evidently broke the lock, which was defective to begin with. The drawer came half-out, and the letter came wholly out." He drew an envelope from his pocket as he spoke. "Here it is."

Taking some sheets from the envelope and unfolding them, he held them near the fire-glow, but on the point of beginning to read he paused, and glanced at Nora Strange. His manner had now lost all its acidity, and his expression was gravely sympathetic.

"I am afraid this will not make very pleasant reading, Miss Strange," he said; "but I have to read it."

"I want you to read it," she answered.

He nodded, glanced across at David, and began:

" 'Dear C.'—C., of course, is Charles Shaw—'Yours just received didn't surprise me. I knew there was trouble brewing, and some of the trouble was with me when your letter turned up. It was H.' H., we will find as the letter continues, is your Uncle Harvey—Harvey Strange. 'He turned up like a bad penny and got difficult. "How much longer is this going on?" he said. "Till you die," I told him. That's the way I've always dealt with him, and as a rule he takes it, but this time he'd got some Dutch courage into him out of a bottle—that man drinks like a fish—and he said that if we didn't let him alone he'd squeal himself. That's the first time in all these years he's adopted this tone, though I've been waiting for it. I know you don't like talking about these things, you're good at stuffing cotton-wool in your ears and shutting your eyes—yes, *you* ought to have been born the girl and me the boy—a lot of use you've been, always keeping out of the way, or putting spokes in! But now things have got to be faced. We've given H. all he can stand and a bit over, and that makes him dangerous. Personally I think he's finished, anyway—he's just a mess'—I'm sorry, Miss Strange, but after all, this merely justifies your father's opinion of his brother—'and he's not been in a fit condition to go to a club for weeks. We've had nothing, as you know, and that's what I got him to come about, because you can be quite sure L. W. left me nothing, and I need it!' You will learn who L. W. is in a moment. 'But of course I didn't expect your letter to come at the same time. It arrived in the middle of our interview, and H. recognised the writing at once, snatched it out of my hand, and opened it himself before I could stop him. So the cat was out of the bag and he knows all about his brother's intended visit, and insists on coming along with me. Because I've got to come. You see, there's more in this than you have any idea of. You didn't know, did you, that——' "

"Wait a moment!" whispered David suddenly,

Mr. Maltby stopped reading.

"Hear anything?" he asked.

"They all listened intently, then David shook his head.

"Sorry, I expect I was mistaken," he said. "Go on, sir. Unless you want a respite, Miss Strange?" he added.

"I don't think there can be any respite till this is settled," answered Nora.

"You are right," agreed Mr. Maltby, and resumed his reading:

" 'You didn't know, did you, that my dear husband wrote to W.S.'—W.S., your father, William Strange—'just before relieving me of his earthly presence?' The writer does not seem to be mourning her dear husband very seriously. 'I found out myself yesterday a couple of hours after burying him, when I was going over his things, and *that's* why your own letter didn't surprise me. God knows what L.W. wrote! What I found was only the beginning of the letter, and as he'd tried to disguise his writing I suppose he wrote anonamously, if that's how you spell it. I expect he wrote another letter after deciding not to send the beginning I came across. Fancy not destroying it! Was there ever such a fool? Of course, he was ill, so that may have been the reason of his carelessness. If ever I marry again it won't be a doctor, and I only married this one because there was a good reason—and at least he had good looks twenty years ago.' Twenty years ago," repeated Mr. Maltby, looking up from the letter, "And a doctor. W. for Wick, eh? The L. doesn't matter. The doctor who attended your grandfather during his last illness—was present at his death—and signed the death certificate. You note, we are progressing! 'But if L.W. was a fool, he was also sly enough to keep a secret, and evidently old J.S. told him one before he popped off so suddenly.' Was J. your grandfather's first initial, Miss Strange?"

"John," she said.

"Thank you. J.S.—John Strange. 'And now he has passed it back to J.S.'s son,' the letter goes on. 'Better late than never, eh? Well, the same applies to *us*! I can't tell you just what the secret is, because the bit of letter I found didn't go quite far enough, but I can tell you this. There's money in it! A lot! In the house! And we've got to find it before W.S. and his precious winner of this week's Beauty Contest do!' That, I take it, is a not very subtle reference to yourself, Miss Strange.

"Now, perhaps, comes the most unpleasant part of this exceedingly unpleasant letter: 'So get ready to see us— H. and myself. It ought to be to-morrow if the snow doesn't delay us.' It did delay them—ruinously. 'But though H. will arrive with me, do we want him to leave with us? Think it over. If an accident happened, and W.S. arrived shortly afterwards, and no one else was about—and *we* won't be about!—well, remember Cain and Abel! Yours, Martha.' Of course Martha Wick, the nurse."

Gravely Mr. Maltby returned the letter to its envelope and the envelope to his pocket.

"Now, if any of us had received such a letter as that," he said, "and if, in the hurry of flight, we had left it behind for the police to find, might we not risk returning to burn it?"

"You—you mean——?" faltered Nora.

"I mean, Miss Strange," replied Mr. Maltby, "that Charles Shaw is absent. That Martha Wick and your uncle are absent. That there is a hammer in the dining-room which has killed a man, and also a chair in which another man died. Never mind for the moment how I know these things. Accept them as facts. And before the next fact comes along we want to know what was in that letter to your father from Dr. Wick. If he is still sleeping, do you feel inclined—in the exceptional circumstances—to see whether you can find it?"

"I'll go up with you," said David, as Nora rose.

"You are on sentry duty," Mr. Maltby reminded him. "However, I will relieve you temporarily—unless Mr. Hopkins would like to do so."

Mr. Hopkins gave no sign of having heard the offer.

CHAPTER XXIII

"ONE WHO KNOWS"

LYDIA looked up from her gloomy vigil as the bedroom door opened softly and David, followed by Nora, came in. David had a nearly-spent lighted match in his hand.

"Anything happening?" she asked.

"Not yet," replied David. "Apart from finding out things."

"Yes, everybody goes on finding out things but me," answered Lydia. "One day, David, you shall tell me a long, long story—meanwhile I've only got a collection of bits and pieces that don't seem to make anything! By the way, have you and I wished each other a merry Christmas? It would be a pity to miss it." She turned to Nora. "David and I always go on like this, but beneath it all we have lovely natures, etc., etc. I suppose you've come for the latest bulletin? Really, I think your father only needs his rest. He's sleeping like a top."

Nora tiptoed to the bed and regarded her father's serene countenance. He seemed thoroughly at peace with the world. Nora's own expression as she watched him was one of puzzled relief.

After a moment or two she turned to a small brown bag on a chair. It was her father's bag, and she opened it, while Lydia threw David an inquiring glance.

"She's looking for something," murmured David.

"Never!" Lydia murmured back sarcastically. "Of course, be awfully careful not to tell me what it is."

"A letter. We're on the track, Lydia—but that story you want is much too long to explain just now. Any luck, Miss Strange?"

She shook her head, and then turned back to the sleeper in the four-poster bed.

"All in a good cause," said David, while she hesitated. "But would you like me to?"

"No—I will."

Her hands moved softly about the sleeper's pockets. In a few seconds she gave a low exclamation as she drew out an envelope. It still retained fragments of a broken seal on the flap, and it was marked. "Strictly Private."

"This is it!" she exclaimed.

"Well done! Then down we go!" answered David. "Come along!"

He opened the door, struck another match, and held it up as Nora slipped out of the room with her find. A moment later, the door was closed again.

"Thanks ever so much," said Lydia.

David and Nora found three silent people waiting for them below, but Mr. Maltby broke the silence with a quick, "Well?" as they reached the hall.

"I've found it," answered Nora, handing the envelope to him.

He took it and returned to the fire, while David resumed his sentry duty by the kitchen door. After regarding the words, "Strictly Private" on one side of the envelope and the broken seal on the other, the old man asked:

"Do you want to read it yourself first?"

"No, I'd rather you read it out," replied Nora, in a low voice. "Whatever is in it, we've all got to know now."

"That is so. The way you are taking this is very helpful. It increases our desire to help you in return. Yes," he went on, as he drew the letter from its covering, "this is obviously the writing of an ill man—and I should say there is an attempt here at disguise. Everything fits." He turned to the end. "Even to the signature. 'One Who Knows.' Well, let us now know ourselves."

Turning back to the first page, he began reading:

"'Dear Mr. Strange,—The writer of this letter wishes to do you a good turn and to relieve himself of certain knowledge before the opportunity to do so slips away. He has possessed this knowledge for many anxious years, and he makes no excuse for having withheld it for so long. If you guess his identity, you may guess also that he has had his cross to bear, even if you decide that he has borne it badly. What he now has to say is the matter of importance, however, and judgment can be left to other hands.

"'You will doubtless recall certain facts regarding the death of your father, John Strange. You will recall that he was ill for some time previously, and that it became necessary to engage a nurse. You will recall that, a few hours before he died, he sent for you and your wife, and you may have assumed that this was death-bed repentance, which, as the writer himself knows, can destroy evil thoughts and can put one in a strange mood. You will recall the circumstances of your father's death. I will not dwell upon these circumstances. You may have formed your own conclusions.

"'But there is something you will not recall, because until this moment I alone have known of it.

"'It was generally believed that your father's fortune was confined to the considerable amount that came to your brother, Harvey, and which was so soon expended in gambling, racing, and other expenditures which I will not mention. But your father, towards the end of his life, had begun to have other ideas regarding his fortune, ideas which in the peculiar circumstances of his position he thought, perhaps, might not be put into execution—and which, as it happened, were not. It was because of this—because of his doubts and also, very probably, his own peculiar disposition, that he contrived to convert a considerable portion of his investments—five thousand pounds—into cash. I myself was merely told, on one occasion which he subsequently regretted, of the existence of this cash. Not of its whereabouts. And I swore on the Bible that I would reveal nothing of what I knew. I claim no virtue for the fact that I might have broken his oath later on to my own advantage. I merely state I did not do so. But now I break my oath, knowing that at this moment John Strange would wish it. And, after all, the money was intended for you, in any case, and had your father lived a little longer, he would doubtless have informed you where to find it.'"

Mr. Maltby, who had read up to this point without pause or interruption, now stopped for a moment and looked at Nora. She was staring at him almost unbelievingly.

"Now you can understand, Miss Strange," said the old man, "why your father came here, and why he said he would be giving up his class in Newcastle."

"But—where is this money?" she gasped.

"That we will find out," answered Mr. Maltby. "Unfortunately, we are not likely to learn from the conclusion of this letter."

He resumed reading:

"'What you will decide to do after receiving this is, of course, your own concern, but should you visit Valley House, the writer advises you to keep your intended visit to yourself and not to let it become known to any one beforehand.' Yes, but your father *did* let some one know beforehand, Miss Strange. He wrote—it seems quite reasonably—to Charles Shaw. He did not know apparently that Charles Shaw would write to Martha Wick. Well, to conclude—there is not much more: 'It would be strange if, exactly twenty years after your father's death, you learned what he then failed to tell you.' Yes, that has also occurred to me. And then comes the somewhat anomalous signature under which Dr. Wick tried to conceal his identity—'One Who Knows.' It is anomalous because Dr. Wick did not know. He merely possessed half-knowledge, which we ourselves must complete." As he pocketed the letter he looked towards the slowly ticking clock, the hands of which were just visible in the firelight. "The twenty years will very soon be up!"

At the kitchen door, David suddenly stiffened.

"Hear anything?" gulped Mr. Hopkins.

"Yes, this time," nodded David.

Mr. Maltby leapt to his side and pushed the door half-open. From the back passage came a sound of shuffling feet.

CHAPTER XXIV
THE RED TRAIL

"In here—quick!" whispered Mr. Maltby.

The three men slipped into the kitchen and closed the door softly behind them. From the passage beyond the dark space in which they stood came the shuffling, hesitating sounds. The sounds had not quite reached the door on the farther side of the room, nor did they seem in any hurry to do so, drawing close gradually, with frequent pauses. Then followed a longer pause than usual. The person who was making the sounds was gathering his courage to open the door.

"Do we wait or rush?" whispered Mr. Hopkins.

It occurred to him afterwards that perhaps he had only thought the question. He did not hear his words, and apparently nobody else did.

Now a new sound broke the silence. The sound of a door handle being turned very, very slowly. Then a tiny creak, and then a vague disturbance of the darkness through which three pairs of eyes were straining. The disturbance was a long vertical streak of dark grey, only just discernible against its background of black, and gradually thickening. As it thickened it became more discernible. It was the widening crack of an opening door.

A long smudge appeared in the streak, then slipped off it into the blackness. The streak itself remained—a faint impression of a passage's dimness—but the smudge moved on, unseen and also unheard. To Mr. Hopkins, waiting tensely for some terrible culmination, it was one of the ghosts he had professed to disbelieve in, about to swoop upon him for his incredulity. He wanted to swoop himself, but he was held motionless either by an old man's will or his own numbness. So, instead, his mind swooped. It swooped for an instant right out of the kitchen into the comfort of Jessie's arms. He dwelt hard on their material warmth, and decided that when all this frightfulness was over he would find those arms somehow. "Be nice to her, too," he decided. "She's a decent little thing—make her really like me, eh?"

But all of a sudden the attractive face in his vision changed. He did not recall the transition; he just awoke to the fact of it. He was staring at another face into which Jessie's had melted. A face with terrified, too-brilliant eyes, that seemed to be staring back right into hell. Mr. Hopkins had never seen such an expression on a human face before, which may have been why for a tottering moment he wondered whether it were human. The hair above the eyes was grey. The cheek below, dead white. A mouth half-open, revealing the small black gap of a missing tooth, did not improve the startling picture revealed by Mr. Maltby's electric torch.

"Don't move," came Mr. Maltby's quiet, stern voice. "You're cornered, Charles Shaw. And you will spend your Christmas in jail, charged with the murders of John Strange and of his son, Harvey."

Then the terrified man found his voice.

"I didn't murder them!" he screamed, as though years of control had suddenly cracked. "It wasn't me, I didn't murder them!"

"Then you had better take this opportunity of proving that you did not," answered Mr. Maltby, "for you will never get a better."

"Who are you?" gasped Shaw.

"It does not matter who I am," replied Mr. Maltby. "Be satisfied that I am not a judge about to put on the black cap. For that is the man you will have to face before long, unless you can clear yourself to me and to those with me here to-night."

David, quickly grasping the situation, had slipped to the farther door, and was standing beside it to cut off the man's retreat if he tried a sudden rush, but Mr. Hopkins still remained motionless, appalled by the fear in front of him, and humiliated by his own. Mr. Hopkins was a slow learner, but to-night he was learning. Whether he would remember his lesson in the morning sunlight was another matter.

The man who had believed himself alone, and who has stolen into an abrupt glare of ghastly publicity, swallowed with difficulty. For a short time, while the others waited, it seemed as though those screamed words had drained him of all others. Then he passed to a new phase. A hopeless depression began to replace the agony of a terror that could not be sustained indefinitely, but that left a chronic, ineradicable pain. The pain, in Shaw's case, was a tight one round the neck.

"What do I do?" he asked, with almost pathetic simplicity.

He had left the rack for the floor of the torture chamber. He just knew he was locked in, and the instruments were all around him.

"Tell the truth," replied Mr. Maltby. "If it damns you, we shall learn it anyway. If it clears you—well, we shall recognise the fact more quickly than a jury. Truth is the world's greatest asset—and the most neglected."

"Where do I begin?"

"How about the autumn of 1917?"

"You know about that?"

"I know enough to ask you for more knowledge. In the absence of more knowledge I must only conclude that it was you who murdered John Strange in this house twenty years ago."

"I never murdered him."

"Well, well, prove it!"

"I can't prove it."

"Then give us an opportunity to form our own judgment. John Strange fell ill. Begin from there. What was the cause of his illness?"

"Weak heart, sir."

"Come, come! I know the death certificate vouched for that, but——"

"You asked what caused his illness, not what caused his death," interrupted Shaw, with a tiny flicker of spirit.

"I concede your point, if you will concede, then, that he did not die of the cause of his illness or, more correctly, the original cause. Heart trouble sent him to his bed. What kept him there?"

"He got worse——"

"Yes, yes, I know that!"

"It was his nurse kept him there."

"Martha Wick?"

"Yes, sir."

"The doctor's wife?"

"Yes, sir. Only she wasn't his wife then."

"I see. She married him afterwards?"

"Yes."

"Through love, or interest?"

"Eh?"

"Well, we will come to that in a moment. What was her name before she married? I thought the doctor might have selected his wife as nurse to give her a job. Were they engaged?"

"No. Not then."

"Then what was her name?"

"Don't you know that?"

"If I do, you shall confirm the knowledge."

"Martha Shaw."

"Shaw!" exclaimed Mr. Maltby. "Shaw! No, I did not know that! But I guessed that. It explains a good deal, Mr. Shaw! What relation was she to you?"

"My sister, sir."

"Your sister? Exactly. Then perhaps it was you who suggested her as nurse?"

"Yes, sir—though I never dreamt what it was going to lead to."

"Was she qualified?"

"She knew a bit about it."

"And you thought that bit enough?"

"Well, I dare say." He shuffled uncomfortably. "Actually it was her who suggested it, and—well, I fell in with the idea."

"Perhaps you have made a habit of falling in with her ideas?"

"That's right. She'd got a will."

"Why did she want the job?"

"She may have smelt something."

"A most expressive phrase. Now tell us what she smelt?"

"Well, after a bit, she saw how things were going," muttered the man. "I mean, when Mr. William came back with shell-shock, and the old man—that is Mr. John Strange—got to hear of it. And then when he also heard about the baby—well, she saw the effect it was having on him. The way he was changing."

"Your sister saw that?"

"Yes."

"How Mr. John Strange was regretting his attitude to his son William, who he had always liked so much more than his son Harvey?"

"Yes."

"And what did his son Harvey think of this change?"

The man's face twitched, and he was silent.

"I appreciate your delicacy," said Mr. Maltby acidly. "Mr. Harvey Strange cannot now speak for himself, and you do not care to talk ill of the dead."

"My God, do you think this is easy?" burst out Shaw.

"I should not think it is at all easy," answered Mr. Maltby, "and I do not see any reason why it should be. What did Harvey think of his father's change? Did it distress him?"

"He didn't like it."

"How did he learn of it?"

"At first, Mr. Strange—the old man—admitted it. Then he shut up."

"Exactly! *He*, too, saw how things were going?"

"I expect he did."

"It is obvious he did. Ill in bed, at first with heart trouble, and then with some other trouble. Yes, that bed must have been a very unpleasant place for him.... We have had some glimpse of the fear that bed stood for—the terror—the pains in the stomach, which has a different geography from the heart. His nurse knew how things were going, and his son Harvey knew how things were going, and I have no doubt his doctor knew how things were going. John Strange had not been quite clever enough in the art of concealing. Nor, later on, were his jailers. A pretty position it must have been, Shaw! And you, of course, merely looked on, eh?"

"You can think what you like," replied the man, "but that's just how it was. I had nothing to do with it."

"Precisely. At that time, as to-day, you refused to face things, and put cotton-wool in your ears and kept your eyes closed."

Shaw started.

"I note that you recognise your sister's phrase."

"Do you—do you mean——"

"That I found the letter you returned here for?" asked Mr. Maltby. "Yes, I found that most interesting document. So, you see, I know quite a good deal before you tell me anything. Poison, was it?"

Perspiration increased on the man's forehead.

"Drop that light a bit, can't you?" he muttered. "You're blinding me!"

"Blindness seems to be your favourite condition—though, of course, more alleged than actual." Mr. Maltby lowered the light to the man's waistcoat. "What kind of poison? Arsenic?"

"It was poison, and the kind don't matter!" burst out the wretched man. "But I had nothing to do with it, as God's above! Why, I didn't even know what was going on!"

"Or suspect?"

"What's one against three? It was the new will they were afraid of——"

"How would that affect your sister?"

"Eh?"

"Do not make me repeat my questions."

"Yes, but what's the use when you know the answers to most of them? She saw her chance, and took it. She—did a deal."

"With Harvey?"

"Who else? She bargained for a share."

"Were you in the deal?"

"No! But—no, I wasn't!"

"Explain the 'but.'"

"Well, Mr. Harvey said—when I got to know—that he'd look after me. Keep me in my job."

"Wouldn't William Strange have kept you in your job?"

"I expect so. There you are! What did I get out of it?"

"What did the doctor get out of it?"

"Oh, he was well under her thumb by then. She could have ruined his practice. You see, I'm not keeping anything back——"

"I wouldn't make a virtue of that," interrupted Mr. Maltby contemptuously. "How could your sister have ruined Dr. Wick's practice?"

"She had him under her thumb——"

"Yes, so you said, but how, how?"

Shaw shrugged his shoulders wearily. "This is pleasant for me, isn't it? If you must know, my sister had her attractions in those days, and the doctor fell for her. Is that enough?"

"You are telling us they had an affair?"

"That's the polite term for it."

"And then—not to continue the politeness—she blackmailed him into complicity?"

"Yes, and after that married him to keep him quiet. Now you've the lot."

"No, not quite," answered Mr. Maltby. "When John Strange, defying his four blackguardly keepers—you talk of one against three, Shaw, but he was one invalid against four—when he cheated them in the small hours of Chrismas morning and struggled down to the hall to spring his surprise upon the company, who was it put the fatal dose in his champagne—the dose that prevented him from completing his speech? *Did you?*"

"I've told you, no!" shouted Shaw.

"And I've advised you to control yourself," answered Mr. Maltby severely. "We are doing so! Who put the fatal dose in the champagne?"

"My sister, damn you!"

"You state that Martha Wick, nee Shaw, murdered John Strange?"

"It's the truth."

"And that Harvey Strange, Dr. Wick, and yourself were accessories?"

"They were, yes, but I wasn't! How many more times am I to tell you that I had nothing to do with it? Even if I'd known I couldn't have stopped them! I knew afterwards, of course, but not at the time. My God, haven't I been through enough to-night? How much longer?"

"That will depend largely on yourself. I assume—correct me if I am wrong—that John Strange managed somehow to make a new will, and that its production was to be one of his surprises, but before he could refer to the new will, much less produce it, he died? You do not correct me, so I take it I am not wrong. Where was this new will? Was it found?"

"Yes."

"By whom?"

"Martha."

"Martha. Always Martha. And Martha is not here to give you the lie. Where did she find it?"

"When he was dead it was her duty to lay him out. She found it in his wig."

"What's that?" cried Mr. Maltby sharply.

"His wig. That's what I said. His wig. He'd written it on thin paper, and that's where he'd hidden it."

"I see—I see! What did Martha do with it after she'd found it?"

"She put it back again, and said nothing till he was buried."

"Why?"

"To continue the blackmail. She told Mr. Harvey later that she'd found it, and if he didn't keep her in comfort she'd reveal it. Then he'd have nothing, because the new will left everything to Mr. William."

"Your sister must be a she-devil, Shaw."

"I'm not denying it," replied the man.

"Of course, since she and the doctor and Harvey had the arranging of everything, and were all of the same mind, they had no one else to worry about. Did Dr. Wick continue his practice?"

"No. He sold it, and they moved."

"And bled Harvey."

"Yes."

"Did you get any of the—blood?"

"If you mean money, no. That is, I just got my wages for my job here."

"What happened when Harvey's money ran out?"

"He learned other ways of making it."

"Your sister saw to that?"

"I expect so."

"For twenty years. Until her husband died. And now Harvey is dead. Who killed him?"

Shaw gulped. His throat was dry, and his faint flickers of spirit seemed to be dying.

"She killed him," he said.

"How?"

"I'm not saying any more."

"With a hammer?"

"My God, what's the use? Did *you* find the hammer?"

"I found it."

"All right. Yes. With a hammer."

"Do you remember saying to me, 'How much longer?'"

"Eh?"

"You can shorten the length by telling me now exactly what happened here this afternoon when your sister and Harvey turned up?"

"You read my sister's letter to me?"

"I did."

"Then you know some money was hidden here? He'd hidden that somewhere, as well as the will."

"I know that."

"We began looking for the money. I didn't expect Mr. William and his daughter till the evening, and even then I thought the weather would delay them, as it had delayed the others. But Mr. Harvey was out to make trouble. He said if we found the money the whole of it was his. Those two quarrelled all right. My sister was mad, and he was drunk, and at last he left the house, just after I'd made tea to try and get back a little peace. He said he was fed up, and was going to blow the whole show. I don't expect he was, but Martha got the wind up. She took the hammer and went out after him. Then she came rushing back—I won't forget it!—and said what she'd done, and that the snow was covering him up. I didn't wait!"

"You fled."

"We both did."

"You did not get far."

"We lost ourselves."

"Then what happened?"

"We managed to get into the barn. It's round the back. I've been there nearly ever since."

"Did you know the house was occupied?"

"We saw the lights. That's why we went to the barn."

"What did you think?"

"That Mr. William and his daughter had arrived."

"They had not arrived. We had, from a snowbound train. Why did you stay so long in the barn? Was it only the weather?"

"No. We wanted my sister's letter. I knew where I'd left it. When the body was found, we guessed the house would be searched, and—well, that letter might have been awkward." He paused, then went on in a depressed monotone, "We wanted to see if we'd left anything else around, too, and to try and get a lie on the position. We decided to wait till every one was in bed. But when Martha thought she'd heard a scream, it unnerved her. She went out—it was quite a while afterwards—after the scream, I mean—I'd tried to stop her—and she didn't come back. I took it that she never meant to come back, or that something had scared her off."

With a sudden shock David realised that the first footprints he had traced had been Martha's, and that if he had continued on instead of turning back he would himself have reached the barn. It was he who had scared the woman away when he had tumbled out of the window.

"But you stayed in the barn?" asked Mr. Maltby.

"Yes, for a bit," replied Shaw.

"Not all the while, then? Between her departure and your coming here?"

"No, not all the while."

"Well, go on."

"I tried to find my sister. It worried me, her not coming back. I thought she might be up to some trick or other—doing something to lay the blame on me. It would be like her."

"She might say the same of you," Mr. Maltby reminded him.

"She might, but she won't," answered Shaw.

"She'll deny your story that she killed John Strange and Harvey Strange."

"I'm telling you, she won't."

"Why not."

"She's dead."

Nothing appeared to ruffle Mr. Maltby, who had kept up his questions with an insistent crispness from which there seemed no escape. He had never once paused in genuine surprise, and though David had noticed the news about John Strange's wig had made a deep impression on him, the interest in this case was less surprise than confirmation. Mr. Maltby had frequently referred to the too immaculate hair in the painting. But now, as he learned this fresh startling fact, he made no attempt to conceal his astonishment. In fact, he raised his electric torch to the servant's face again, as though to seek evidence of the man's truthfulness. The evidence was clearly written on Shaw's features.

"Dead," repeated Mr. Maltby, after a long pause. "Martha Wick is dead."

"Yes," muttered her ungrieving brother.

"And Dr. Wick is dead, and Harvey Strange is dead—and the three dead musketeers cannot deny the words of the living fourth, who now charges them with crime."

"I told you before I started that I couldn't prove anything," said the man. "Now you know the reason."

"And who killed your sister?"

"I didn't."

"I asked you who did?"

"I don't know."

"You came upon her dead?"

"She was alive when I came upon her."

"Alone?"

"I didn't see anybody else."

"Just you two, but you didn't kill her."

"That's right. I've never killed any one."

"Go on."

"I will if you'll let me. I saw her, but she didn't see me. It was along a lane. She was coming back. At least, I thought she was, and I waited, but she took a turning that was between us, and then I realised that she wasn't coming back, and that she probably hadn't seen me because I was under some trees. Or else she might have been coming back till she saw something else round that corner. I don't know. What's it matter, anyway?"

"What did she see round the corner?"

"A car."

"Well?"

"In a ditch."

"Why, that must have been——" began David involuntarily, and then stopped.

"Do *you* know anything about that car?" asked Shaw, in obvious surprise.

"Whether he does, or whether he does not, is beside the present point," interposed Mr. Maltby. "Continue, please."

"P'r'aps it isn't beside the point!" retorted the man. "Still, let's get it over! It was a closed car, with one window open. Looked like a derelict, otherwise I expect she'd have given it a wide berth. Even as it was she went up to it cautiously enough—of course, I was coming along again by then, though she still hadn't seen me yet.... My God!"

Suddenly he laughed. It was the only laughter they ever heard from him, and they would have been better without it. It contained the chill and mockery of death, and formed the grimmest moment in the whole grim memory, apart from that first moment when the electric torch had developed his terrified face like a suspended, neckless head in the blackness.... The laughter ended as abruptly as it had begun, and the dull monotone continued:

"There was somebody in the car. Hiding. Don't ask me who or why. We neither of us knew while she tiptoed up to that open window. She was right next to it before she got a glimpse. She thought it was me. Funny, eh? She thought it was me. Have you got that? She thought it was me. And she poked her head at the window, and she said, 'So that's where you're hiding, you bloody murderer, well, you can stay there while I fetch the police! Because you did it, see?'

"Then a hand shot out of the window, and a knife went clean through her face.... Next thing I remember, I was outside here."

"So *that*," murmured Mr. Maltby, in a voice so low that it was scarcely audible, "is where Smith comes in!"

CHAPTER XXV

TWENTY YEARS AFTER

"Miss Strange!"

Lydia's voice came down the darkness into the hall, but only Jessie heard it. Nora's ear was plastered against the keyhole of the kitchen door.

"I think you're wanted," Jessie called softly, and Nora turned as Lydia's voice sounded again.

"Miss Strange! Can you come?"

Nora groped her way quickly up the stairs. Her mind, like her body, was groping through the darkness—groping to steady itself in a whirling world. At the top of the stairs she felt a hand take hers and give it a hasty little squeeze.

"Your father's waking. I think he ought to see you first, but I'll be just outside if you want me," whispered Lydia.

"Yes—thank you," murmured Nora, and slipped into the bedroom.

In the glow of the fire she saw her father raising his head from the pillow, and she was beside him in the chair lately occupied by Lydia before he realised that any one else had been in her place. He smiled as he recognised her, and then his eyes roamed slowly round the shadowed room.

"Well, Nora—we're here," he said. "As I said we should be."

"Are you feeling better, dear?" she asked.

"Oh, yes. I have had a refreshing sleep. And you?"

"I'm quite all right."

"That's good. And that young fellow who brought us here?"

"He's downstairs, with the others. You remember, I told you——"

"Yes, I remember. I remember what you told me. I saw some faces before the explosion."

"Explosion, dear?"

"It was a snowball. It came over from the enemy lines. And then I went to sleep, and now I am awake again, and I feel considerably rested. How long did I sleep?"

"Not very long."

"How long? What's the time? Light the lamp. There used to be one—yes, there it is, on that table. Then we shall be able to see the time.... This is very peaceful."

Nora hesitated. Then, remembering that there was no longer any need for darkness, she went to the lamp and lit it. She only just managed to repress a shudder as the room glowed into clearness and she thought of a former occupant of the four-poster bed.

"Thirteen to two," she said, glancing at her watch.

"Then in thirteen minutes ... A happy Christmas, Nora. And it will be. I don't quite understand all these other people, though. But then, after all, one understands nothing."

"They were snowbound, as I told you——"

"Yes, yes. A train. That was not what I meant. Where's Charles?" As she did not answer at once, he added, "The servant here. He used to be a good chap, Charles. He was very upset when I went to the front. But weak—that was his trouble—and after I left I don't believe your Uncle Harvey ... However, we will not talk about your Uncle Harvey. Is Charles here?"

"I—don't know," she murmured.

"Don't know——?"

"I mean, yes. That is—yes, he's here."

"I am glad. I had an idea something was said—but, of course, he should be here. I wrote to him. And he was here twenty years ago."

"Father, don't you think you'd better try and go to sleep again?" asked Nora anxiously.

"Sleep again?" exclaimed William Strange. "Indeed not! I have just woken up. What's the time now? Twelve minutes to? At this time, twenty years ago, I was down in the hall with your mother. Waiting." He sat bolt upright and suddenly gazed at her. "Have I ever told you, Nora, how like your mother you are? She had your same—how can one express it?—the same fragility. But strength, too. More strength than you. No one knew how I had to fight her to get her to marry me after the family had disapproved of the match. She only consented when she was convinced that I needed her.... Well, for those four years, I think she was happy ... Nora! I feel I should not be here! I should be downstairs—somebody else should be here in this bed——"

She laid her hand gently on his arm.

"Do go to sleep, dear," she begged.

"No, no, I must go downstairs! I must hear what he——" He laid his free hand on Nora's, and patted it. "Don't worry, my dear. There is something I want to say to you. As a rule, one is dumb—there is a wall between what one knows and what one can express—but to-night it is easy. You struggle and fret till the tide gets you.... This is what I want to say. We are not free agents, you know. My father disliked this philosophy, for he had a strong will, though it was forced underground, and he liked to think it was his own property. That was our only serious difference, apart of course from my marriage—and perhaps that was due more to others than himself. But what has happened had to happen, and what will happen must happen. What we call good and what we call bad are merely the reflections of our personal desires and hatreds. That is where our criticisms are at fault. Criticism is the one thing I cannot understand. In the war, I hated! Then a shell exploded everything, and left the useless husk you have known…. But I went on…. Only in a different world…. I suppose you understand nothing of what I am saying? It is unimportant and trivial?" His voice wavered suddenly, as though doubts had come to him. "We must get down," he muttered. "Please do nothing to prevent me. Your mother always knew what was best for me, though she fought me till she was certain. I am afraid I made a poor return."

"Yes, of course we must go down," answered Nora, giving up her protests, but dreading what they would go down to. "And I do understand. I'll help you out of bed…. No, wait just one second, will you? Only a second. Then I'll do everything you want."

She ran from the room, closing the door behind her. To her relief she found Lydia outside.

"No need to say anything," whispered Lydia. "I've been a pig in a good cause, and listened. Go back—I'll let them know."

"Yes, please do! One day I'll thank you," murmured Nora, with more gratitude in her voice than her words could express. "But I must warn you of something—they've caught Shaw!"

"My dear," retorted Lydia, "do you think I'd turn a hair by this time if they'd caught the King of Zululand?"

Back in the bedroom Nora found her father waiting for her patiently, and she felt that his patience was due to his faith that she would make no more difficulties. She helped him from the bed, and put on his boots—the only clothing that had been removed. They were warm and stiff, from having been dried before the fire.

It was four minutes to two when they left the room. The passage was dim, but light came up from below, and as they reached the top of the stairs they heard voices. The voices ceased as they began to descend. Nora wondered what was going to be the end of that short, queer journey, and what strange expectation of her father's would be fulfilled or disappointed. All she knew definitely was that something was going to happen. She had no idea what it was. Nor had she an idea that Mr. Maltby had been preparing for the moment before he received Lydia's warning.

If her father shared her ignorance, he gave no sign of it. He accepted the situation with the same uncanny obedience that had characterised his attitude when help had suddenly arrived at the stranded car to guide them on the last stage of their journey. Watching him, Nora recalled his recently spoken words: "What has happened had to happen, and what will happen must happen." He was living his philosophy.

It was also, apparently, the philosophy of the old man who stepped forward from the motley gathering to greet them.

"Good-evening, Mr. Strange," said Mr. Maltby. "I am glad you have come to join in the Christmas toast—which, of course, would have been incomplete without you."

"Thank you," answered William Strange, and walked to a position near the front door.

"That is where you were standing?" asked Mr. Maltby.

Mr. Strange nodded gravely.

"But your wife was by your side? Am I right?" Mr. Strange nodded again. "Miss Strange, will you stand by your father?"

She took her place quickly, while her heart thumped.

"There were also four others present," went on Mr. Maltby. "Three of them—Harvey Strange, Martha Shaw—as she then was—and Dr. Wicks we need not resurrect——"

"They were by the dining-room door," said William Strange mechanically, as though he were reciting a lesson.

"Will the rest of you stand by the dining-room door, then?" asked Mr. Maltby. "In this case I will not perform the unsavoury act of allotting parts. The fourth was Charles Shaw." He paused for a moment, then turned towards the kitchen, and called, "Charles! The champagne! For a health!"

Everybody stiffened at that call saving William Strange and the old man himself. Nora's heart thumped harder than ever, and David, watching her from the dining-room door, fought an almost uncontrollable impulse to go to her side. Instead he performed the Christian act of patting another hand that was nearer to his. "But for that," ran Jessie's diary subsequently, "I should have *died*!" Neither William Strange nor Mr. Maltby, however, showed any nervousness. Both were smiling—the former contentedly, the latter with a kind of whimsical irony.

The kitchen door opened, and Charles Shaw appeared with a tray. On the tray were wine-glasses and an opened bottle of champagne. More nervous than anybody, yet obeying his strange instructions as a drowning man catching at a straw, he had possessed the forethought to set the glasses well apart; otherwise, his trembling hands would have played a tune with them.

"Thank you, Charles," said Mr. Maltby. "Kindly fill our glasses after we have each taken one."

While the queer ceremony was being performed, the old man looked at the clock, moved a little nearer the painting of John Strange, and then glanced at the lamp close to his hand. His own glass was filled last. An empty one remained.

"You, too, Charles," he said.

"Me, sir?" muttered the man.

"Why not?"

Shaw filled the empty glass. Then they all waited, while Mr. Maltby again looked at the clock whose ticking was now the only sound in the hall. One minute to the hour. The minute seemed an hour itself. When it had passed, and the clock gave its preliminary wheeze before chiming, Mr. Maltby raised his glass in his right hand, and cried:

"A happy Christmas to you all, and a toast to——"

The clock chimed two, and as it did so Mr. Maltby's left hand moved swiftly to the lamp and turned it out. Immediately afterwards a ray of light, directed by the same hand, illuminated the face of the picture, seeming to transform it into a living thing. Even the voice that followed through the darkness appeared to issue not from the lips of Mr. Maltby, but from the lips of paint.

"... My granddaughter, Nora Strange," said the voice. "But before you drink I have certain observations to make. And, after all, since you have already been kept waiting twenty years, to wait a minute or two longer now will make small difference.

"The first observation relates to my new will. This rests with me beneath my wig, and since it is now only of academic interest, perhaps it can continue to rest with me there. It was intended for you, William. From my wig it should have been transferred to your hands for safe keeping, for by its terms it left everything to you and nothing to your brother Harvey. But Harvey is now dead, the victim of his own and other people's avarice." The voice paused, to allow time for this news to sink in, but only one tiny gasp came through the darkness to register its reception. "Therefore, what is left of the property reverts to you, in any case, for you may be sure that if Harvey himself made any will, which is doubtful, it will never be produced in a Court of Law.

"The second observation relates to certain other property. Wills have a distressing habit of being lost, stolen, misinterpreted or upset. To upset my own will, my eccentric habits might have been quoted to prove that I was not sane when I made it. I assure you I was quite sane. I was so sane that I converted five thousand pounds of my money into banknotes—and my intention, William, was to tell you privately where those notes were. Perhaps it was as well that I did not. Perhaps even those notes would have been cheated from you. Now they are still intact—where I originally hid them. And like my will, they are concealed by my wig. But they are not beneath the wig—they are behind it—behind the wig at which you are now staring. The wig of paint."

Again the voice paused. And again there was a little gasp. This time it came from Shaw. The voice continued:

"How different you are, William, from your brother! Harvey would not have waited, as you are doing. He would have flung himself at the picture, smashed it, as he helped to smash the original, and torn at the frame!

"I have but one other subject to mention. Charles Shaw.

"Three people, all now dead, combined to poison me. Was Shaw a fourth, or was he an unwilling accessory before—or after—the fact? Did his sister, who poisoned me physically, poison her brother spiritually, as she poisoned her husband? And if this is so—if Shaw's offence does not go beyond a contemptible and blackguardly weakness—is he a fit subject for forgiveness now that his evil influences are removed? Could such a man wipe out his past by service?

"If, William, you decide that he could not, then you will let matters take their normal course. But should you decide that he could, then there might be no need to reopen the question of my murder. One murderer has died a natural death. The other two have themselves been murdered—Harvey by Martha Wick, and Martha Wick by, perhaps, the hand of Providence. We might accept that hand.... Good-night, William.... A happy Christmas."

The light vanished from John Strange's face, and a prosaic old man struck a match, relit the lamp, and raised his glass.

CHAPTER XXVI
THE OFFICIAL VERSION

"WELL, boy, this is the ruddiest Christmas morning *I've* ever spent!" exclaimed the inspector, shoving his notebook aside. "Four murders in a dozen hours! I reckon I've earned my bit of turkey."

"Three murders, begging your pardon," replied the sergeant. "If I hadn't sent him over the edge he'd have knifed me."

"Well, we won't hang you for yours," grinned the inspector. "Just the same, I wish we'd got our man alive—he deserved the rope, if ever any one did!"

"Personally, I'm all for saving trouble," answered the sergeant, grinning back.

"Oh, so am I. But I'd like to have heard that man talk."

"Jibber, you mean! He was running amok—off his nut!"

"You can learn something even from a lunatic."

"But you've got it all straightened out, sir, haven't you?" asked the sergeant.

The inspector pulled the notebook towards him again and opened it.

"Yes, I think so," he said, turning the pages. "Yes, I expect so. Thanks to the assistance of that fellow Maltby—whose statement was of more use than all the rest put together. Clear-headed chap, that. He helped me work out Smith's movements from A to Z. Let's run over 'em again, and you see if you can trip me up. I'd sooner you did it than somebody else! Now, then. Smith steals Barling's letter-case in the train. Barling attacks him, and Smith strangles Barling. Murder No. One."

"O.K.," nodded the sergeant.

"Not for Barling," commented the inspector grimly. "K.O. for him. Right. Smith bunks, gets to Valley House, loses the letter-case there, plays hide-and-seek and ducks-and-drakes and God knows what, is suspected by the company—also off that same train, of course—and finally, when challenged, does another bunk. Meets Harvey Strange on his way to Valley House——"

"What was Harvey going there for?"

"To spend Christmas there, of course! What else? Smith has another rough-house——"

"Why?"

"Don't you know?"

"No more do you, sir."

"Quite correct. Now you see why I wish Smith were alive, so we could make him speak. But it's a fairly easy guess how that second tussle started. What condition was Smith in when you met him? You said he was off his nut yourself."

"So he was."

"All right, then! He bumps into Harvey Strange, Strange says, 'Hallo, what's the hurry?' or something of that sort, and Smith doesn't wait to explain. Don't forget, they saw him go off with the knife and the hammer, and they heard a scream——"

"Yes, and we've got the knife, but where's the hammer?"

"Buried in the snow somewhere, I expect. We'll find it."

"I've thought of another idea, sir," said the sergeant.

"What is it?"

"Smith had lost his letter-case, so he needed more cash for his getaway. With one murder against him, he might have risked a second for another wad of notes. You can only hang a man once."

"That's a good theory of yours," said the inspector. "We'll note it. It could fit Murder No. Two. But it doesn't fit Murder No. Three, though."

"We don't need it for No. Three, sir, do we?"

"No, we don't. By that time Smith was completely dippy. You can keep steady after one murder, but a couple's a bunch. After Murder No. Two he hurries on. He passes William Strange and Miss Strange in their stranded car——"

"Why doesn't he go for them?"

"Let him rest occasionally!"

"Yes, p'r'aps his arm was tired."

"And there were two of them. Seriously speaking, I don't see any flaw there. Miss Strange asks him for help, and he says he'll fetch it. But, of course, he doesn't. And the next glimpse we get of him is on the way to Hemmersby, where we've been notified of the murder of Barling—Murder No. One—and are on the look out for the wanted man. Police-Constable Lake spots him, challenges him, chases him, and loses him. Smith turns back the way he came, hides in the car—we found his cap there afterwards, you remember—and stays there till Martha Wick passes by and becomes too inquisitive."

"Or p'r'aps he dived in the car when he saw her coming," interposed the sergeant, "and she hadn't the sense to leave it at that."

"Sergeant," said the inspector solemnly, "if you're not very careful, you will become intelligent, like me! That is probably what did happen—though, frankly, all this 'probably' and 'possibly' is getting on my nerves. Anyway, Smith knifes the poor woman in a fresh panic, and commits Murder No. Three."

"What was Martha Wick doing out so late?" asked the sergeant.

"Martha Wick was the sister of the manservant at Valley House," answered the inspector; "and she was on her way to help cook the Christmas dinner.... Finally, Smith had the bad luck to meet *you* on the edge of Webber's Dip, and you refused to become his fourth victim. Quite rightly. But you can be ready for a nice little spot of bother over that." He rose and stretched. "So that's that—for the moment—and now for the next. Strictly speaking, sergeant, it's not our job to phone up relatives and make other people's excuses for 'em, but as there's no telephone at Valley House and Christmas comes but once a year—thank God!—I suppose we must allow this exception, eh? Where are those four telephone numbers?"

CHAPTER XXVII

JESSIE WINDS IT UP

AT half-past seven on Christmas night Mr. Hopkins descended from the bedroom he had been allotted jointly with David, and reached the hall just as Mr. Maltby was coming out of the drawing-room.

It was a very different hall from the hall the stranded party had entered some twenty-eight hours earlier. After the most disturbed night any of them had ever spent, and a morning almost equally disturbed by a succession of snow-covered police officials—the great snowstorm had ended, but the aftermath would remain for many a day till the peaceful white mantle changed to brown slush and the brown slush oozed unpicturesquely away—Lydia had gripped the situation once more and organised a decorating expedition. Death lay around the house, but Life had to fight it, and in this case Life had the advantage of being no poorer by the Death. So the afternoon had been spent in clearing the front door and in making short excursions into the woods, from which holly had been wrested and cleared of its white covering. The house was now bright with red berries and glistening, prickly leaves. The brightest berries and the best leaves had been reserved for the frame of John Strange's picture.

Then the guests, no longer uninvited, had retired to their allotted rooms to make what toilets they could; and Mr. Maltby and Mr. Hopkins had been the first to descend.

"Going along well?" inquired the latter, as the old man closed the drawing-room door.

"Mr. Thomson will soon be fit to continue his broken journey to his aunt," replied Mr. Maltby, "who will complete his return to depressed normality."

"Well, we've all had broken journeys, come to that," commented Mr. Hopkins.

"And shall continue to have them," answered Mr. Maltby. "There is no such thing as a destination."

Mr. Hopkins cleared his throat. Pity this old man couldn't talk rationally, like an ordinary human being. Nasty habit of making you feel inferior and uncomfortable. Still, Mr. Hopkins was not likely to see much more of him, and meantime there were one or two points that might be cleared up while the opportunity remained.

"Cigar?" said Mr. Hopkins.

"I am allowed my pipe," said Mr. Maltby.

They lit up. Suddenly Mr. Hopkins shot his first question.

"How did you know those notes were stowed away behind that picture?"

"It was an easy guess," answered Mr. Maltby.

"Nobody else guessed it!"

"No. The spectator sees most of the game. The players are often blinded by its details."

"Can't see the wood for the trees, you mean?"

"Precisely."

Mr. Hopkins replaced his cigar between his lips, then took it out again and regarded the ash.

"And there was nothing else, eh? Just that, eh?"

"What else do you mean?"

"I mean—well, the whole thing was so damn queer. It—it *was* you speaking, wasn't it? I mean, damn it, of course it was! But it was, wasn't it?"

"If I told you that it wasn't," answered the old man, "if I told you that I did not say a single word through my own initiative, but that my lips moved in obedience to the spirit of John Strange, would you again say, 'Bosh'?"

"I—I don't know!" murmured Mr. Hopkins, uncomfortably.

"Then why should I take the risk of inviting your contempt?"

"Oh! Yes, I get you. Well, no, I—well, no, I wouldn't."

"You now believe, then, in ghosts?"

"Come, I haven't said that!"

"But you are ready to believe in them?"

"Ah, that's different! I might be."

"Bosh, Mr. Hopkins," smiled Mr. Maltby. "And it is a pleasure to make the remark to one who has exploded the rope trick. You recall certain observations of mine in the train? Probably you were not listening. I have a respect for those who believe in ghosts, and one of my best friends is convinced that he is on excellent terms with a man who looks once a month for his head. But that is not my personal way of explaining the apparently unexplainable, and certainly the ghost of John Strange has not been here this Christmas—fortunately for John Strange. We hatch ghosts in our own minds, out of the logic that is beyond us. Logic, through science, may one day recapture the sounds of the Battle of Hastings, but this will not mean that the battle is still going on. Believe me, Mr. Hopkins, there are quite enough astounding, uncanny, mind-shattering experiences within the boundaries of sheer logic to eliminate the necessity of ghosts for our explanations or our thrills. We are only touching the fringe of these things. We have only touched the fringe of them in this house. There has been no ghostly hand to guide me."

"Then what the devil did you mean when you took me up about 'running the show'?" demanded Mr. Hopkins. "I said you were doing it, but you gassed about—about something bigger!"

Mr. Maltby gave a little shrug.

"In the minute sense, perhaps I did run the show. Perhaps I even enjoyed it. It amused my analytical sense—especially the final scene last night—or, rather, early this morning—and the entertaining interviews with the police. Probably I like showing off, in my particular way, as much as you do in your particular way.... But it was only in the minute sense. How can I explain what I mean by the larger sense in a way that will leave you any wiser?" He paused. "Have you ever wondered how two butterflies, fields apart, can find each other? How thousands of bees, lacking our alleged intelligence, return in the evening to the same hive without any map or clock to guide them? How trees grow in all sorts of shapes, but always with balance? How separate drops of water merge into communal obedience to a mass of dead matter called the moon, and go for six hours one way and then for six hours another? Have you ever wondered how the Inevitable You came about? ... You cannot explain these things. You can only become conscious, at rare moments, of the working of some vast Arrangement, and that consciousness may be due to your own intensive vision, or to the simplicity of the view you happen to be travelling through. The view *we* have just been travelling through was so simple and neat and orderly that one almost felt the vast Arrangement was tired, or on holiday, and wanted a little easy recreation."

"I suppose you know what you're talking about?"

"It is clear you don't."

"I don't!" admitted Mr. Hopkins. "But I'll risk one more question all the same!" He stopped abruptly as the kitchen door opened, and Charles Shaw carried a tray into the dining-room. "*Him!*" whispered Mr. Hopkins. "Why all the white-washing stuff?"

Mr. Maltby waited till the servant had passed back to the kitchen.

"If there is any white-washing of Charles Shaw, he will have to do that himself," he replied. "My remarks last night concerning him were made in deference to my reading of William Strange's desire. William is growing old, and he is a sentimentalist. He will be far happier forgiving Shaw than imprisoning him. Moreover, quite a lot of soiled linen need not now be made public. William Strange and his daughter deserve a little peace, don't you think? And Shaw's curse is weakness—cowardice—not deliberate wrong.... Or do you think Shaw murdered John Strange?"

"No, certainly not," answered Mr. Hopkins.

"Or Harvey Strange?"

"No."

"Or his sister Martha?"

For an instant Mr. Hopkins's eyes popped. He stared at Mr. Maltby.

"I hadn't thought of that!" he exclaimed.

"I had," replied Mr. Maltby. "We only have Shaw's word for that incident. He could have done the murder himself—given the pluck and the motive."

Mr. Hopkins shook his head.

"Can't see him having either," he answered. "No, I don't think he did it."

"And I am sure he didn't. So all we have to worry about is the adding of Harvey's murder to Smith's score, instead of to Martha's. Both now dead themselves. To descend to an expressive vulgarism, I should worry!..."

On the landing above two other people were not worrying. David had deliberately lingered after Mr. Hopkins had left him, and was standing in the passage when Nora came out of her room. She smiled when she saw him, but did not pause until she found him standing in her way.

"Don't go down for a moment," he said.

"Why not?" she asked.

"Because I've been standing here for six and a half minutes especially to talk to you, and I should hate to have wasted all that time for nothing."

"What do you want to talk about?"

"I've forgotten, though I knew all the while I was waiting."

"Perhaps it was to say a merry Christmas?"

"We've said that dozens of times."

"Well, you'll think of it later. I want to go and see how father is."

"Your father's all right," he retorted. "He's got five nice, crisp thousand-pound notes, and a daughter, so you needn't worry about him any more. Try thinking about somebody else for a change. Of course, you wouldn't have the kindness to ask 'Who?' would you?"

"If you like!" she laughed. "Who?"

"The Man in the Moon," he laughed back. "It's a damn good thing for you we couldn't find any mistletoe. Come downstairs, and I'll show you some string tricks."

"You are ridiculous! I've got to help your sister in the kitchen!"

"No, *you're* ridiculous! First you say you've got to go and see your father, and then you say you've got to help my sister in the kitchen. Well, I say you've got to see my string tricks!"

"Are they good?"

"I don't know—I've never done any yet...."

"I heard them laugh as they went downstairs," ran Jessie's diary, "and I said to myself, 'There goes *your* little romance, Jessie,' of course it was silly, because there never was any romance, I mean only in one's mind, but if there had been I'd have said good-bye to it because I knew how things were turning out.

"Then I thought I'd go and see how Mr. Strange was myself, as Nora hadn't gone. Of course I didn't listen to their conversation, but I heard it as I was just coming out of my room myself, only I waited so as not to interrupt them. It gave me a funny feeling when I knocked on Mr. Strange's door, because that was the room I had had first, with the four-poster bed, he'd wanted me to go back to it, but I said I wouldn't dream of it, and I wouldn't!

"I called out to know how he was, and he asked me to come in, so I did, and we had rather a funny two or three minutes not quite knowing what to say, but somehow it was quite friendly. I could never be really at home with a man like that, though, as he lives in another world or seems to. Then suddenly he said, 'Well, shall we be getting down?' And then I said, 'Yes, let's,' I've come to the conclusion that real conversation isn't half as clever as you find in books or plays, anyhow mine isn't, and then we went down.

"Lydia was in the kitchen, and David and Nora were off somewhere or other, I don't know where, and as the three other men didn't need me, or if Mr. Hopkins did I wasn't looking to see, I thought I'd go in and have a word with poor Mr. Thomson, who one felt rather sorry for, being out of it all, though there was some of it he was well out of!

"I was glad I went in as soon as I got in, because he looked so very white, though better, and pleased to see me.

" 'How are you?' I said.

" 'Getting along fine,' he said. 'How's your foot?'

" 'Oh, that's almost mended,' I said, 'I don't think it was ever as bad as I thought it was.'

" 'I bet it was,' he said, 'people often crick their ankles badly at the time, but get better quickly, it's the difference between a strain and a sprain, I've a cousin who's a chemist.' Then suddenly he went red and asked out of a clear sky, 'I say, you know you're really awfully decent, you don't mind my saying that, do you, it doesn't mean anything, but may I ask you something?'

"I began to feel a bit red myself, all I'd done was to pop in and give him a cheery word now and then, knowing it was what I'd have liked in his place.

" 'Yes, of course,' I said, hoping it wasn't what I thought, though I don't know how one could have thought it with Mr. Thomson.

" 'Have I made a fool of myself?' he asked.

" 'Gracious, what makes you think that?' I exclaimed.

" 'I don't know,' he replied, 'but have I?'

" 'Of course you haven't,' I said, 'you've been ill, no one can prevent that, but if you'd been well you'd have helped as much as anybody, I remember, you began doing everything.'

"There was something quite pathetic about him, and I expect that's what made me say, almost before I knew it, 'Shall I have my Christmas dinner in here with you?' His was to be brought in, and it seemed rather a shame he should be all by himself. He didn't believe I meant it first, I hadn't, but when he saw I did he almost blubbed, and I had to pretend I didn't notice. Of course, he wasn't well.

"And then the gong went, and so that's what happened.

"I stayed with him till dinner was over—he wasn't allowed much of it, poor fellow! And I could see him falling in love with me, it's awful, I get all the wrong people. I mean, he's all right, but goodness! ... Anyway, I couldn't help it, could I,

I was only trying to be kind—as David had been to me. And then I joined the others, leaving the door open so he could hear, and we drank healths to everybody under the sun. I can't stand much wine, which I expect was why I ended up by proposing the health of the police inspector! I can't stand much—oh, I wrote that.

"Well, anyhow, we'd been through hell and it was Christmas, so if one or two of us did get a bit funny, well, who could blame anybody?"

THE END